The Long Trail

At seventeen, Dot Pickett is young to be taking on the role of trail boss on a cattle drive. But Dot's life has been hard, and he has become brave, resourceful – and occasionally ruthless.

Now he has successfully led a cattle drive from Texas to Kansas and is setting off for home with the saddle-bags of gold owed to the Texan ranchers. But Dot has fallen foul of a notorious outlaw family and he knows that they will try to ambush him. Then when Dot goes to the aid of a young woman, the gold disappears and he embarks upon a quest to retrieve it.

Dot's search takes him on a long trail of danger, deception and intrigue, leading him from Abilene deep into the bayous of Louisiana, where his courage and determination are pushed to the extreme in order to survive and reclaim the cattlemen's gold.

Dedication

To my mother, Mildred Marie (Armstrong) Shanks, God rest her soul, who was always there for me, and now so sadly missed. Also, to my sister, Anya Eakins, and my brother, Les Armstrong, who are always there now. This book would not exist, nor would I, were it not for these three. And lastly, to my daughter, Karla Paola Caldera Gonzalez, and my three grandkids, Mildred, Maite and Romina. *Te amo*!

The Long Trail

John Armstrong

A Black Horse Western

ROBERT HALE

ISBN 978-0-7198-2457-9

The Crowood Press
The Stable Block
Crowood Lane
Ramsbury
Marlborough
Wiltshire SN8 2HR

www.bhwesterns.com

Robert Hale is an imprint
of The Crowood Press

Typeset by
Derek Doyle & Associates, Shaw Heath
Printed and bound in India by Replika Press Pvt Ltd

CHAPTER ONE

'Mister, I may be only seventeen, but don't let that stop you. If you think you can ride this bronc, just shake out a loop and put your spurs on!'

I stepped back from the bar and faced him squarely. He sat his drink down and looked at me, the laughter gone from his face.

'You made the brag, mister,' I said to him again. 'Now go ahead and pin my ears back.'

He looked at the crowd, who had backed away from the bar. Licking his lips, his eyes met mine and in them I saw him for what he was.

Some men were braggarts, men who talked big and liked to swagger around using brash language and rough ways to bull their way through life. The man before me was one of these and now that he'd been called, he didn't quite know what to do.

Myself, I was just a youngster, fresh up the trail from Texas. But I was not the wet-behind-the-ears boy that this man had taken me for. I carried a gun on my hip and I didn't carry it for show. The butt was of walnut, worn smooth by the fit of my hand and I could make that old gun speak – six words at a time, and each spelled death.

When I came to this bar, it had been to relax and have a

drink. The ride up the trail from Texas had been long and hard, hot and dusty. We'd swum swollen streams and dodged bars of quicksand, fought off Indians and battled jayhawkers trying to cut our herds.

My riding partner had been gored to death by a bull and our trail boss had been killed by a Kiowa arrow. All in all, when we finally hit town, we were in no mood to fool around.

I came here to the Alamo Bar for a drink. When I was through, I would go to the Drover's Cottage and meet Brice Fellows, the cattle buyer contracted to buy our herd. He had done business with us before and would be expecting us soon.

I had just ordered my drink when the stranger lit in on me. I tried to ignore him at first, having had my fill of trouble on the trail. But well enough he could not leave alone. He fancied himself a big man with a gun and thought he'd have a bit of fun with a cowboy from Texas.

He went on about this and that, cussing every Texan who had come up the trail and allowing as to how they all needed their ears pinned back. Finally, I had taken enough and pushed away from the bar.

I laid it out plain to him then, calling his hand, and it took him by surprise. I reckon he felt confident that in his own town and in his own saloon a body would back down from him and all his bluster. He'd figured wrong with me; I didn't give a damn as to whether I killed him in here or dragged him outside and killed him. Either way was the same to me.

Unable to hold my eyes, he looked down at the floor, then back to his friends scattered a safe distance away from him.

'No call to get riled, stranger,' he said defensively. 'A little funnin' never hurt no one.'

'Then you've never been "no one",' I said. 'You mentioned

something about pinning some Texan ears back. Now you've got your chance. You take it or take yourself out of my sight.'

A look of indignation crossed his face and he replied angrily, 'I'll do no such thing! You're a stranger here and a Texan on top of that. If anyone should leave, it's you. We've had enough of your kind around here.'

He looked at the faces throughout the room but could find no support among them.

'You'll find no help there, mister,' I said, causing him to look quickly back at me. 'You bayed this coon, now you shake him out'n the tree.'

His hand hovered above his gun butt and his fingers twitched nervously. He wanted to draw – so dearly he could taste it, but when the good Lord had passed out gumption, this man hadn't received a full ration.

A way out – that's what he was looking for, and I was of a mind to give it to him. Softness was no part of my make-up, but truth be told, I just didn't feel like taking the bother. A shooting in town would mean an inquest and maybe a day or two in the calaboose. I had better things to do, like sell the herd and collect the gold for it. There were folks needful of that money; folks who'd risked everything they had on this herd. Their livelihood and their very lives depended on the returns from this cattle drive. And now that the boss was dead, it was up to me to get the gold back to them.

Like I said, I had better things to do than tom-fool around with some wanna-be badman.

'Mister,' I said seriously, 'I've got other steers to brand. Your best bet would be to join your friends and let the hair of the beast grow long. If you persist in this, they'll be dragging you out of here by your boot straps.'

Before he could answer, I reached up and backhanded him across the face. Instinctively, his hand went to the stinging on his cheek. When it did, I reached out with my left hand and slipped the pistol from his holster. As quick as that he found himself covered with his own gun.

'Move away from the bar,' I said, motioning to an unoccupied table behind him. 'You have a seat over there and contemplate the error of your ways.'

He moved to the table and sat down, his face red – not so much from the blow I had given him, but from his own anger and shame.

I reached into my pocket and flipped the bartender a two-bit piece. 'Give him a drink on me,' I said. 'And when he's cooled off, you can give him back his gun.'

I slid the pistol across the bar and the bartender snatched it up. Pulling my hat down tight on my head, I looked once more around the room before I turned and left it behind.

So this was Abilene. There was a lot I had heard about this town, but I had never been here myself. Each of the past two years I had been up the trail with herds from Texas, but we had taken the Western trail on up to Dodge City. This was my first time to Abilene and it was said that Wild Bill Hickok himself was the marshal. From stories I'd heard of him, a body had best step careful in Abilene.

I was in a hurry to meet Brice Fellows and strike a deal, but first I wanted a hot bath and a shave. Those things were unheard of on the trail and that couldn't be helped, but anytime a man had the chance, he should be clean-shaved and bathed. Least ways, that's what I believed, although I'll admit I didn't have a lot to shave.

Our herd was bedded down outside of town. On our arrival, there was a good five thousand head of cattle scattered around and about the outskirts of Abilene. I would 'spect most of the drovers were now in town, as I'd never seen such a passle of folks in all my days. They were everywhere! Punchers with their fanciest duds on, all decked out to cut a dido in town.

There were cattle buyers, too, in their houndstooth suits and string ties. They walked the streets in a grand manner, some smoking cigars and tipping their hats to the ladies.

There were Indians about, also. Some dressed like the white man and others bedecked in their native garb. I was wary of Indians myself, as my pa and ma had been killed by them whilst I was a youngster. But these in Abilene seemed peaceful enough.

As I rode up the street, I passed Henry's Land Office and the Metropolitan Hotel. Further down the street was the Twin Livery Stables, and it was there that I pulled up. A man named Gaylord took my horse and to my question of a good place to stay, he named the Drover's Cottage and the Metropolitan.

Most folks had heard about the Drover's Cottage. A man named Joe McCoy had built it, stocking it like the fancy hotels back east, with the best of wines, whiskeys and cigars. The rooms were said to be plush and the help courteous and kind.

I was a down-to-earth person myself and although the Drover's Cottage was the biggest thing in town, I thought I would prefer the Metropolitan.

Stabling my horse, I headed back up the street to get a room. On the way I ran into Slim Hite, one of our hands.

'Howdy, boss,' he said. 'Where 'bouts you headin'?'

'Fixin' to get a room at the Metropolitan. Once I get cleaned up I'm going to find Mr Fellows. The sooner we sell the herd and get shut of Abilene, the better I'll feel.'

We walked a few steps together up the street, each of us taking in the sights of a booming cow town.

'I'm going to Fisher's,' Slim Hite said invitingly. 'Want to come along?'

'No, thanks,' I said. 'You go ahead. Maybe I'll join you later.'

He turned and sauntered off, the boots on his bowed legs beating a quick tattoo on the boardwalk.

Fisher's Addition was a part of Abilene that held the honkytonks and was sometimes referred to as the 'Red Light District'. You could get most anything there, from cheap whiskey to shady ladies, and most of the punchers made a beeline for the bars and dives that made up Fisher's Addition.

It was also the wildest part of town and many a shooting and stabbing happened there. Hickok would be there, I assumed, making sure things stayed as quiet as possible and knowing the man, I knew it was a task he was well qualified for.

No sooner than the thought of Hickok came than I saw the man himself walking slowly down the street. Although I had never seen him before, I knew him instantly. He was a tall man with a drooping mustache that was neatly trimmed. He sported a black hat and wore a finely tailored black suit. He had two pistols on his person, but didn't carry them in a holster like myself and many others; he wore them tucked in a broad sash that went around his waist. And if ever a man had the look of knowing how to use them, it was he.

As he drew close, his eyes measured me with a calculating glance. His eyes were hard, but not mean. He tipped his hat to me and spoke as we passed, a pleasant-seeming man to me. Not at all what I had expected from the stories I had heard of him.

When he was gone, I entered the Metropolitan and walked up to the front desk. A man with glasses and a handlebar mustache was busy at his ledger. Seeing me, he looked up from what he was doing.

'Howdy, friend. What can I do for you?'

'I'd like a room,' I answered. 'Nothing real fancy, just plain and simple.'

'All right,' he said. 'How long will you be staying?'

'Hopefully just a night or two. But if I need longer, I'll let you know.'

He turned the ledger to me and pointed out a line for me to sign on. When I had spelled my name out, he handed me a key to room nine and looked down at the ledger.

'Up the stairs and to the left, Mr Pickett. If you need anything, just give a yell.'

I thanked him and turned to leave when he spoke again.

'Dot Pickett?' he said reflectively, rolling my name in his mouth. 'Are you the Pickett from Doan's Crossing?'

I turned and looked at him cautiously, but his face was innocent.

'I am,' I answered. 'Do you have business with me?'

'Oh, no, Mr Pickett. I only recognized your name on the ledger. The story of your ... "difficulties", shall we say, is well-known in Abilene.'

'Do tell,' I said coldly. 'That's in the past, my friend, and best left there. I have business to conduct here.'

'You watch yourself, then, Mr Pickett. Two of the Banks boys are here in Abilene. Caxton and Everson. Caxton,' he went on, 'he's the smart one of the bunch and by far the most dangerous.'

Doan's Crossing was on the north side of the Red River, across from Texas and in the Oklahoma Territories. John Doan had opened a store there on a natural crossing of the Red. He sold supplies and most anything a person needed. Any herd coming up the Western Trail had to cross at Doan's and although bars of quicksand were abundant, a safe crossing could be made were a man careful.

Last year on a drive for the Ten Bar, we had camped at Doan's after crossing the Red. I was sixteen then and it was there that I killed my first man. Or men, I should say.

There were five of them when I entered Doan's, all bunched at the bar and drinking rot-gut whiskey. They were a sorry looking lot if I ever saw one and I ordered a drink at the far end, away from them.

Outlaws, jayhawkers and baldknobbers were aplenty these days and unless I missed my guess, these boys were a little of each. What they were doing this far south I couldn't say, but their business would always be questionable to honest folks.

We had been short of hands on that drive and those we had had stayed with the foreman and the herd, sending me on over for supplies.

Johnny Barnes and Sandy Carson were two of the five. The other three were the Banks brothers: Ed, Dawson and Lenny. They asked about our herd and where we were heading. To be courteous I told them, and they then turned out to be full of questions, seeming mighty interested in our herd and our men.

Finally I left, having purchased the supplies we needed. Later that day and close on to dusk, the same five men rode out to the herd, joined by two others whose names I never knew.

Our trail boss was Phineas Dalton, from Austin. He was an older man and a good man, but a little too soft to deal with men like these.

We rode out to meet them, Phineas and I, and they claimed to be inspectors of some sorts, saying that without a certificate of inspection we could proceed no further. They also claimed to have authority to inspect every herd of cattle for proper ownership and that the cost of these services would be ten cents a head.

Our herd then had numbered just over two thousand and at ten cents each, we couldn't afford to pay. They then offered to take a percentage of the herd instead, for this so-called 'inspection certificate'.

12

Mr Dalton balked at this suggestion and the conversation turned nasty. I sat quietly, taking everything in, but also kept my hand close to my gun.

Suddenly, Dawson Banks drew his gun and shot Phineas from the saddle. I returned the fire instantly, killing Dawson and then Ed with my first two shots.

Phineas was a game old man and from his place on the ground he opened up. For what seemed like minutes, but was actually only seconds, shots filled the air with a deadly boom. Horses were rearing up and some were bucking in half-jumps across the land.

Lenny Banks went down, as did Sandy Carson. I emptied one gun then drew another, barely missing a count as I fired again.

A bullet from someone's gun hit my saddle horn and whined away nastily. Another clipped my ear and one tore at my shirtsleeve. I fired away regardless, continuously pumping rounds at the 'inspectors'.

Johnny Barnes was dropped by Phineas, and the two whose names I hadn't known turned and spurred their horses away as fast as they would go.

Our herd was not the only at Doan's that day and the shots from our set-to started a stampede, both herds mingling together and charging east along the Red River. We lost at least a hundred head – fifty or so in quicksand and fifty more in the river. Three days it took to round up the herds and another day to separate them. It had been quite a bother and a lot of hard work.

In the meantime, Phineas Dalton was taken to a doctor back on the Texas side of the Red and the three Banks brothers were buried in shallow graves, their names burned on makeshift crosses with a running iron.

Johnny Barnes survived his wounds and slipped away in the night. Where to, nobody knew, but he was never seen again.

Once more we hit the trail, as the news of the gunfight preceded us. Seemed like the Banks brothers had been pulling their inspection bit on other herds coming up the trail and folks were not unpleased to hear of their demise.

My name was thrown about and when we at last arrived in Dodge City, I was a known man. I found it bothersome and had been glad to be out of there.

The reputation of a gunman was nothing I wanted, but nonetheless it was now attached to my name. Even the man here in Abilene had recognized it and I reckoned that it would be that way from now on; there was nothing I could do about it. But the thing I found most disturbing now was the presence of Caxton and Everson Banks here in Abilene. Now was not the time for trouble with the likes of them.

Caxton and Everson were not brothers to the three from Doan's Crossing, but were cousins. A better stripe of men, yet outlaws just the same. If we were to cross paths there would be trouble for certain, and that I wanted to avoid. I had hoped that selling the herd and taking the gold back to Texas would be a quick and simple thing. Now it was beginning to look as if just getting out of town alive would be a chore in itself.

CHAPTER TWO

Later that evening, I ordered a steak at the Drover's Cottage. It was, in fact, a fancy place; the fanciest I had ever seen. It was packed, too, and I found the atmosphere to my liking.

The food was excellent and plentiful, but I found the wine a bit weak for my taste, never having tasted wine before.

I ate slowly, savoring the food and watching the people come and go. When I came in I left word for Mr Fellows at the bar. Now a slim, fifty-ish man was heading my way.

I stood as he approached the table and he asked questioningly, 'Mr Pickett?'

I nodded and we shook hands. 'I'm Brice Fellows,' he said, friendly. 'Is Cole with you?'

'No, sir,' I answered. 'He was killed by Kiowas down the trail.' Cole Benson had been our trail boss on the drive. I had been up the trail to Dodge with him once before. 'We buried him where he lay,' I finished, 'on the open prairie north of the Salt Fork.'

Brice Fellows' expression turned sad and he looked away momentarily. After a minute, he turned back to me.

'Cole was a good man. Did business with him many times. Are you the rep, then, for the herd now?'

'That I am,' I answered. 'And if it's my age that bothers you, don't let it. Young though I may be, I've been up the

15

trail and through the woods.' Slicing off a piece of steak, I chewed and swallowed before explaining. 'We lost three men on the way up. Tom Tucker was my riding partner and second in charge. We lost him under the horns of a loco'd bull. When it came down to it, in the end I had more trail savvy than the others, so I took up the harness. We made the rest of the drive with no trouble and no loss of beeves. Now all that's left is to strike a deal with you and get back to Texas.'

We talked on about cows and cattle drives, drinking coffee and haggling over a price for our herd. Finally a deal was struck, and a fair one it was. We would get fourteen dollars a head. Mr Fellows offered a draft on a bank in San Antonio, but the folks that owned these cows were a long ways from there. They wanted gold and I intended to see they got it.

'Will you be leaving soon?' Brice Fellows asked.

'As ever as I can,' I answered.

'How many hands do you have?'

'We came up the trail from Texas with twelve, counting myself. There's only nine left now, but of those only two will be going back to Texas with me.'

'You'd best keep a sharp eye out then, son. You'll be carrying a lot of gold and there's a lot of unsavory characters between here and Texas.'

'We'll be careful,' I said. 'Thanks just the same.'

He was right about the gold. If word got out that we were carrying fourteen dollars a head, times almost two thousand in gold, every crook in Kansas would be on our trail. That was a sight of money. More than any I had ever seen before. That gold would be my responsibility and folks would be counting on its deliverance.

The quickest route back would be straight down the Chisholm Trail. That would also be the most obvious and in a town like Abilene, where every deal and transaction would be known sooner or later, it wouldn't hurt to do the unexpected just in case someone decided to try and take the gold. I was not a trusting soul, nor was I a gambler. If I could help it, I wouldn't be taking any chances on getting that gold back to its rightful owners.

It was dark as I walked down the streets of Abilene looking for Slim Hite and Gunner Walls. It was my intention to leave town early in the morning, just as soon as I picked up the gold. The boys would be sore, as they had looked forward to a few days in Abilene, but they'd just have to get over it.

Lights still shone from the windows of most places as I headed for Fisher's Addition. Flynn's, Downey's, The Bullshead and the Alamo Bar, where I had been earlier – I checked them all, finding Slim drinking in Downey's. He was halfway on a drunk and having a good but rough time with some punchers gathered around the bar. He was put out at the idea of leaving bright and early, all right, but he agreed to meet me at the stables come sunup.

Gunner Walls was another story. I could find him nowhere and I searched high and low. The last place I looked was Flynn's and not finding him there, I stayed for a drink.

This place was crowded, too, and doing a booming business. Poker tables were going full bore and whiskey was disappearing by the gallons. Smoke filled the room, and to be heard a person had to yell, and there was plenty of that.

I was on my second drink when a man who looked familiar came in and joined a poker game. Easing over to the table, I watched as they played.

The man with the familiar face won most of the hands and the more he won, the more he loosened up. Soon he was in good spirits and had most of the money in front of him. The others began to drop out; most busted out of the game, others just giving up until another day.

I couldn't place this man, but his face did look familiar. Once, he caught me looking at him and flashed a smile full of teeth at me and winked, enjoying to the fullest his run of luck.

Another man joined the game and I recognized him immediately. It was the man from the Alamo Bar of earlier that day. His face was slightly discolored from where I had struck him and when our eyes met, an ugly grin was on his face. He stared a moment at me, then back to the man I had found familiar.

'So we meet again,' he said haughtily, feeling very smug for some reason. 'Care to join the game?'

'No, thanks,' I said stiffly.

He ignored my brusqueness and continued. 'Why, aren't you a poker player? Seems to me this would be just the game for you.'

'Leave the man be, Boston,' the familiar man said. 'If he doesn't want to play, that's his business. Besides,' he finished, 'the man's lucky for me. I've been winning ever since he came over.'

At this remark, the man called Boston burst out laughing, his whole body shaking with some secret mirth.

'What the hell's so funny, Boston?' the familiar man asked, half-angrily. 'You gone loco or something?'

'No, no!' Boston replied, choking over his laughter. 'It's just the thought of this man being lucky to you.'

'What the hell's so funny about that?'

'Well, you see,' Boston answered, 'I met this man earlier in the Alamo. Had a bit of a disagreement, we did. Kept an eye on him after that and followed him to the hotel where he took a room. I didn't know his name, but I was curious as to who he was.' The man laughed again before going on.

18

'You see, knowing this man's name makes his being lucky to you awful damn funny.'

The laughter left his face then and he said, with a feeling of triumph, 'I think you two gents should meet each other.' He paused, looking back and forth between the two of us. 'Caxton Banks,' he said to the familiar man, 'meet Dot Pickett. The Pickett from Doan's Crossing!'

The man's face turned to stone as he heard my name and his eyes filled with hatred. Instinctively, my hand went to the butt of my gun, but Caxton Banks neither moved nor spoke; he just sat there, staring.

As suddenly as it had appeared, the hate and anger left his face to be replaced by a bland look and I knew that before me was a Banks more dangerous than those I had dealt with at Doan's. Most men were hotheads who let their tempers get the best of them. Caxton Banks was different. He was cold and calculating and in control of his emotions. A man like that would be one to take a man to the limits in any type of confrontation.

Finally he spoke, and when he did, his voice was calm and controlled.

'So, you're the one who killed my cousins?'

'I had no choice,' I answered. 'They came hunting it.'

He looked at the man called Boston, then back to me. 'Be that as it may, they were still kin.'

I didn't answer and a flash of anger crossed his face again. 'I set store by those boys,' he went on. 'They were stubborn and bullheaded to boot, but in spite of that, they had more coming to them than what they got.'

'There's some that'll argue that,' I said.

He looked at me thoughtfully, his face serious. 'I reckon there is, but there's those who'll question anything a man does.'

I didn't answer again while he continued to stare at me.

The men around the table were fearful of doing or saying something that might precipitate a gun brawl. Even the man called Boston was silent, his face tense now and a bit nervous. If guns were drawn and a shooting commenced, he would find himself in a most untenable position.

'So, where does this leave us, Caxton?' I asked. 'Those boys may have been your kin, but they were trying to rob us of our herd. On top of that, they drew first, shooting our trail boss from the saddle without warning. Had I acted any slower they would have shot me, too. Not to say they didn't try anyway.'

'You must be pretty fast,' Caxton said, changing the subject. 'Dawson was as good with a pistol as most and Lenny close behind. Is it true there were just the two of you against the five of them?'

'There were seven of them,' I answered. 'Two ran away when the guns started banging.'

He thought about that for a moment, his eyes finally turning from my face. A minute he sat like that, staring blankly down at the table before him.

The man called Boston became agitated, his hands wringing nervously, as Caxton sat unmoving.

He stood up then, Caxton did, and did he make a wrong move, I'd shoot him. His hands rose to his vest and, removing a cigar from the pocket, he bit off the end and lit up.

A puff of smoke floated lazily towards the ceiling and he watched its slow path upward, his eyes locked on the smoky circle. When it was gone, he turned back to me then his gaze shifted to my right. A man was walking towards us, his step slow and deliberate. Six feet away he stopped and I looked at him, as did Caxton. It was Hickok and he said nothing, taking in the situation with a practised eye.

Caxton Banks turned back to me then, a blank look on his face. 'Be seeing you around, Pickett,' he said. 'Take care of yourself.'

With that, he collected his money and walked straight out of the bar, never once looking back.

I turned my gaze to Boston and he rose quickly, following Caxton's lead. When he was gone, a collective sigh of relief came from the men at the table, one picking up the cards and shuffling half-heartedly.

I moved from the table and over to the bar. Hickok followed and I offered to buy. He nodded and the bartender set them up.

'You having trouble with Caxton?' Hickok asked.

'Not of my choosing,' I answered. 'My name's Pickett. Dot Pickett. The man called Boston sprang an introduction on us unawares.'

'Aw, so that's it,' Hickok said, suddenly seeing the whole picture. 'That sorta clears things up. You be careful of Caxton and his brother. They're not like their cousins. These boys are mean and capable. I've got nothing on them myself or I'd have run them out of town long ago. You remember one other thing, too. This is my town and I'll have no trouble here that doesn't end with me.'

'If there's trouble, Marshal, it'll have to come quick. I'm pulling out of town first thing in the morning.'

He seemed satisfied at that and, finishing his drink, he moved off across the room. As I looked after him, a hand slapped me roughly on the back. I turned and drew in one motion, my gun out and level. There before me was Gunner Walls, a devil-may-care look on his face.

'Damn you, Gunner,' I said, truly angry. 'One of these days you'll get yourself shot full of holes pulling a stunt like that!'

He just stood there, grinning, for all the world looking like a boy pleased at the stunt he'd pulled. Shaking my head, I left the bar, Gunner Walls close on my heels. It had been a long day and if I didn't lie down soon I'd be asleep on my feet.

CHAPTER THREE

Dawn was a short ways off when the three of us saddled our horses and mounted up. Gunner Walls rode with a glum face. He was packing a headache big enough for the three of us. Nonetheless, he had been up and waiting at the stables.

Abilene lay quiet in the early morning dawn. There were a few people around, but not many. An oldster stood on the boardwalk in front of the Emporium sweeping methodically with a beat-up broom. He paused to look up at us as we rode by, then went on about his business.

Brice Fellows was true to his word. He stood waiting for us in front of the bank. We tied our horses to the hitching rail and entered the bank.

A man named Gattis met us inside; a short, portly man with thick-lens glasses perched on a bulbous nose. He wore a suit, and a gold watch fob showed on his vest. If a person were asked to give a description of what a banker would look like, this man would fit that picture perfectly.

Slim Hite and Gunner Walls waited at the door while Mr Gattis showed us to his office. There was no nonsense about the man and he had a certain gruffness about him that I disliked.

Pulling out a strongbox, he began laying out sacks of gold

on his desktop. Brice Fellows went over them, checking the contents of each.

I had never seen so much gold all to once. It fair took a man's wind and I watched humbly as Mr Gattis and Mr Fellows pushed a receipt book to me for my signature. Book learning was not a strength of mine, but with an effort I could spell out my name. I took the pen and carefully printed out each letter. When I was finished, I returned the book to Mr Fellows. He handed the book to the banker then turned back to me.

'That's a lot of gold to be carrying, son. I would advise you to be very careful on your way back to Texas.'

'I will at that,' I answered, running my fingers over the sacks of gold. 'I never asked for this responsibility, nor did I want it, but now that it's mine, I'll take every precaution to see it through.'

I placed the sacks of gold in my saddle-bags, which I had brought along for that purpose. When loaded, they were heavy, but not unmanageable.

Brice Fellows held out an amount with which to pay off the hands. They may be put out at our hasty departure, but they would understand the need for it. Most of them would be going west over the Oregon Trail with good breeding stock for ranchers in Wyoming, Idaho and Montana. I would have preferred keeping a few of them to ride back to Texas with us and the gold, but any time a cowhand could get a riding job, he had best take it.

Gunner opened the door and we stepped out and on to the street. To our left, lazing on the boardwalk, were three men – three men who hadn't been there when we first arrived.

As I threw my saddle-bags on my horse and tied them down, they walked towards us. Without their seeing, I slipped the thong from my six-gun, ready if the need be.

I knew the man in front; he was Caxton Banks. With him was his brother Everson, and a man I didn't know.

Gunner and Slim moved back towards the walk and slightly away from me. Caxton saw this and only smiled, looking at them and then back to me.

'Howdy, Pickett,' he called, as if we were old friends. 'What have you got in the saddle-bags?'

'Never you mind what we've got, Caxton. You keep your nose in your own business and you'll do just fine.'

He laughed and looked around at his cronies, who laughed along with him.

'Why, we were only trying to be neighbourly. Thought we might help you with your bags. They do look a bit heavy.'

The three of them laughed again, enjoying their cat-and-mouse game. I didn't believe they'd try anything here in the street – not necessarily because it was Abilene, but because Abilene was Wild Bill's town. Nonetheless, it angered me that it was now known we were carrying gold, and a good bit of it. These men knew how many cows we had arrived with and they would know the current prices on the market. They would therefore be able to calculate to within a few hundred dollars just exactly how much gold we had and for that much gold, men like these would do more than murder. But not here, and not right now.

Caxton Banks was no fool. He knew we had the gold and he knew we had to get it back to Texas. He also knew that it was a long ways from here to Texas and most of it through a rough and lawless land where a man could die or be killed in any number of ways. I could see the wheels of his mind turning and in his mind he knew his time would come. He was in no hurry, and for now he was content to play the big man in front of those with him.

Brice Fellows came out of the bank then, and glancing at both parties, he hurried up the street. What did he have to do with this? I wondered. Anything? I doubted it. He was a cattleman and a businessman on top of that. He had also had dealings with our trail boss in the past and had proven himself there.

What about the banker? He could have tipped Caxton off that a transaction in gold was about to take place. I hadn't cared for the man from the start and I didn't have much trust in bankers anyhow. Well, that was no never-mind now. The damage was done and that was that.

I threw a leg over my horse and motioned at my men to do the same. Caxton Banks only watched, the smile still on his face.

'You boys be careful,' he said. 'I would be some disappointed were something to happen to you.'

They guffawed again and I replied, 'I'll just bet you would, Caxton, but don't hold your breath waiting. Others of your kind have concerned theirselves with our business and all it did was buy them a grave at Doan's Crossing.'

The smile left his face and his eyes filled with hatred. A hot, burning hate, and for a minute I thought he would draw. If he did, I would put one right in his brisket.

He controlled his emotions and only stared at me, his heart saying one thing and his brain another. We left them that way, three sullen men staring hatefully at our backs as we rode down the street.

Caxton couldn't resist getting in the last word and he called after us, 'Be seeing you, Pickett. Yes, sir, we'll be seeing you down the trail!'

We rode southeast out of Abilene, staying on the flanks of herds that grazed away from town. It was a narrow trail we followed – one that wove haphazardly through thickets of blackjack bushes and sumac. Tangles of blackberry bushes dotted the land and prickly pear grew here and yon.

This was a wild, rough land, brown and sad beneath the sky. Grama grass grew through here, but for the most part it had been grazed out by the many herds that had passed through on the way to Abilene.

All day we travelled, with a wary eye on our back trail. We saw no one, but a time or two I saw dust rising in the distance. A dust-devil mayhap, blown rambunctiously about, but I had a feeling it was more than that. Were I not wrong, it would be men; men who were following us.

The blackjack thickets here were almost impenetrable as far as the eye could see, but finally we found a place to camp. It was a good camp, too, with cottonwoods, blackberry bushes and persimmon trees spread along the banks of a lazy stream. There was a meadow of fine grass as well, and firewood aplenty.

It was a secluded spot, this camp was, and anyone riding up to us would be seen while still a safe distance off. It was this that I liked most, as from now on we would have to be ever alert. Caxton Banks would be coming and he would be coming to kill.

Slim Hite built a fire and Gunner Walls set in on fixing something to eat. I was uncomfortable, myself, and prowled among the cottonwoods along the stream.

If I figured right, Caxton Banks would expect us to head straight down the Chisholm Trail and back to Texas as fast as we could go. I didn't believe they would make their move until we had passed Newton and Wichita and had entered the Oklahoma Territories. That would be the place, I felt, as the only law there was the US Marshal and his deputies. They were kept plenty busy with the Cherokees and the white man was generally left alone.

The trail we would have to follow was through open country for the most part, with only a farmhouse here and there. Places for ambush would be many and even robbery through sheer strength of numbers would be possible. The more I thought about it, the more I disliked it. If we followed the Chisholm – or, as it was sometimes called through the Territories, 'The Osage Trace' – somewhere along the way we would have to meet up with Caxton and his bunch. He could bring as many men as he felt he would need and being there were only the three of us, our prospects wouldn't be good.

That was it, then. We wouldn't do the expected. Caxton Banks would be sure of our returning to Texas by the shortest and most logical route. All of his plans would be centered on that surmise, but if we acted contrary to his preconceived idea, possibly we could throw them off, maybe even lose them completely. We would have to act fast, though, and we would have to act now.

When I walked up to the fire, they stopped what they were doing to look up at me. Squatting on my heels next to the fire, I explained my idea to them. At first they were skeptical, but as I went on, they warmed to my plan.

Soon it was settled. We would not follow the Chisholm Trail. We would slant easterly, short of Newton, and make for Fort Scott on the Kansas-Missouri border. There we would trade for fresh horses and ride on until we hit the Arkansas River at Fort Smith.

Once there, we would sell our horses and board a riverboat down the Arkansas River to the Mississippi River and on into Louisiana. With a little luck, by then we should have left Caxton Banks and his men far behind.

CHAPTER FOUR

We rode hard throughout the afternoon and evening, twice crossing the trail of cattle herds and mixing our tracks with theirs.

Night came and we stopped for an hour on the northeast bank of the Grand River. There we rested the horses and drank coffee that Gunner Walls had 'stewed'. It was best to come to the fire barefooted when he put on a pot, as one cup of his coffee would sure 'nough knock your socks off.

We saw no sign of pursuit on our back trail, but just to be on the safe side, we rode through the night. At dusk we came upon a farmhouse and swapped our three horses for three fresh ones. I threw in a pound of coffee to top off the deal and after sharing breakfast with the man and his wife, we were off again.

We were a tired and sleepy bunch, yet we pushed on nonetheless. If Caxton Banks and his boys had trailed us out of Abilene – as I'm sure he had – then he would be wondering what had become of us. It was likely that he had sent riders on ahead in hopes that they could waylay us as we rode up to them. Once he reached those men and neither hide nor hair had been seen of us, they would know that somehow we had given them the slip. By that time there wouldn't be a lot they could do. Oh, I'm sure Caxton would be some kind of riled and he might send his boys casting about for word of us, but they would find nothing. They might even continue down into the territories and maybe even go as far as Doan's Crossing, but once they went that far and still there was no sign of us, surely they would turn back. There would be no point in pursuing us into Texas, as the Rangers wouldn't stand for a bunch like that at any rate.

It never paid to underestimate a man, though, and when it came to almost thirty thousand dollars in gold, a body could never be too careful. The man at the Metropolitan had said Caxton Banks was the smart one of that lot. How carefully would he have made his plans? Undoubtedly he would expect us to return to Texas the way we had come. But would he have made allowances for any deviation from that course? How much warning had he had that we would be carrying gold, and had he taken the time then to look at every possible route we could use to return to Texas?

I doubted it, as Caxton Banks had struck me as a small-time crook with a small-time mind. But like I said, it never paid to underestimate a man, especially when the penalty for such a mistake would be death.

Fort Scott was dark and silent when we rode in a day later. A man named Givens owned the livery and stables. He was an old, wiry ex-buffalo hunter and it had taken me upwards of an hour to talk a trade with him. He could see our horses were beat and that we had been pushing them hard. He was of no mind to make a swap easy, but the upshot of it was he got our horses, ten dollars and an extra pistol I had in my bedroll.

He agreed to let us throw our blankets in his barn for the night and hung around as we settled in. He talked and watched at once as I unsaddled, and when I hefted off the saddle-bags, his eyes perked up. It was heavy and hard not to show it, but he made no comment.

'You boys rest easy,' he said. 'Don't get a lot of folks through here after dark. You won't be disturbed till morning.' He talked on about this and that, but finally drifted off to his own bunk around back.

It was Slim Hite who brought up Caxton.

'Do you think we've lost them, Dot?' he asked. 'We've come a far piece and nary a sign of them.'

I tossed in my blanket, smoothing out the lumps of hay beneath me. 'I'd say it's a good bet we have. It would have been nigh impossible to follow our trail through those herds. We'd best keep a sharp eye out, anyway. Caxton Banks isn't the only one who'd slit our throats for that gold. There's plenty twixt here and home that'd jump at the chance.'

Gunner Walls was already asleep, with Slim Hite shortly behind. Sleep did not come easy to me, though, and I lay listening to the sounds of the night.

Somewhere not far off, an owl cast its eerie call into the night. Down the street a dog barked briefly and a door slammed shut.

My mind returned to our discussion of earlier that day. I had never been on a riverboat before, but had heard tell of them. A sharp lot of gamblers were said to travel them, playing cards around the clock and not overly particular as to how they separated a gent from his wallet.

There were thieves aboard, also, and pickpockets and thugs. But there would be decent folks, too, and just plain people coming and going. I was anxious to be on that boat, for the sooner we got shut of Kansas the better I'd feel. Not that I had anything against Kansas, but there were those who had desires against me.

I dozed off at last and slept brokenly. Slim snored away in the stall next to me. But it was not his snoring that awakened me; it was the sound of a step. A step made by a man not wanting to be heard.

Silently, I slipped the blanket away and grabbed a hold of my pistol.

Again I heard a cautious step. It came from the back end of the stables. Someone was coming towards us and he didn't want it to be known.

Rolling noiselessly over in the hay, I crouched along the wall of the stall. Peering through a crack in the wall, I could see nothing but shadows. Yet, after a while one of those shadows moved – and moved closer to me.

It was a man, then, and I saw him clearly. He was a stranger to me, but he was no stranger to the rifle he carried in his left hand.

He was slinking towards the stall I now crouched in while his eyes were intent on where I should be sleeping. As he drew closer, I could see his right hand and see it plainly. He carried a knife in it, cutting edge up, and it was a long knife.

He moved on and as he closed upon the front of the stall, he was all eyes for my saddle and gear. I watched his eyes search among my things, seemingly looking for something in particular. Was this one of Caxton's men, or was he someone the hostler had sent for my saddle-bags?

I cocked my pistol to his left and he stopped, like a barefoot boy stepping on a prickly pear. I spoke then in a barely audible whisper.

'Friend, I reckon you've come far enough. It's not polite to go sneaking about in the dark, especially when folks are trying to sleep. My suggestion to you would be to move along while you're still able.'

He didn't move nor speak, only standing there like a silent statue.

I went on, 'You lay that rifle on the ground in front of yourself and the knife alongside of it. Just one false move and you'll have a hole from one ear to the other.'

Slowly, he lowered his weapons to the ground and lay them there, turning his head in an effort to get a look at me.

'Don't bother,' I said. 'The only face you'll see tonight will be the face of death.'

With that, he stopped and directed his gaze back to the floor.

'Who sent you here?' I asked. 'Who put you on to us?'

He didn't answer.

'You come of your own,' I asked again, 'or did someone send you?'

Still, he didn't answer and I gave up, too tired to tie him up and beat it out of him.

'All right, then, you get on out of here and don't come back. Next time I won't be so easy.'

He stood a moment, not sure if I was finished.

'Go on,' I said. 'Get while the gettin's good.'

No one disturbed us the rest of the night and I slept fitfully, glad of the much-needed rest. Dawn rolled around and I was first up, with Slim and Gunner close behind.

The old man from the night before was nowhere to be seen as we pulled out bright and early. I had a feeling this was on purpose and probably for the best, at that. No man likes the thought of another sneaking up on him while he sleeps.

We breakfasted at an eatery on the outskirts of town and then rode on. Fort Smith was due south of us and it was there we would board the riverboat.

The land was flat and gentle where we rode and we made good time, passing only a farmhouse here and there and once a traveling party of Cherokees.

Soon, Baxter Springs was behind us and we crossed into the southwestern tip of Missouri and on into Arkansas. Rain

fell upon us as we neared the Arkansas River and all afternoon it fell hard and incessantly. It was a wet camp we made
that night, but by first light it had cleared.

Gunner Walls was the one familiar with Arkansas. He had
family here somewheres and it was he that spoke as we
neared Fort Smith.

'Sam Peters will take our horses. He owns a place on the
Arkansas River out of town aways.'

He led off and we followed as he talked.

'This is Judge Parker's town. You've heard of him haven't
you? They call him the hanging judge and it's said he's sent
more men to the gallows than anyone else. It wouldn't do to
have a difficulty here. Like as not a man would end up
stretching a rope.'

Peters took our horses all right, and was mighty fair about
it. I wasn't a man who liked being afoot, but for now it could-
n't be helped.

The river was a busy place these days and we booked
passage at the mouth of the Poteau River where she joined
the Arkansas. It was a small steamer we rode, but the food
was good as we set up to the table. They had menus, they did
– a card with all the dishes they served printed up on it. Now,
I hadn't much schooling, and studying over that menu was a
chore, but I got her done and we all ate hearty.

It was noon a few days later when we transferred from our
upriver steamer to a larger one that would take us down the
Mississippi. The waves thrown up by the paddle wheels were
hypnotic to me and I watched absentmindedly. Slim was
resting in the cabin and Gunner was off someplace of his
own.

It took a moment for me to see the small boat that suddenly appeared alongside the steamer. Two men were in it,
one rowing and the other a passenger. I watched silently and
it was a bit later that the dip and splash of the oars ceased as

the boat pulled alongside of a keelboat moored below us. It was then that the passenger left the boat and boarded the steamer. As he did, his face turned upward and I saw him clearly for the first time. It was the man from Fort Scott, the man who had tried to slip up on us in the stables. Now what the hell was he doing here?

Gunner walked up beside me and we stood watching the water pass us by. I told him of the man boarding the steamer and how I suspected his arrival as no coincidence. He agreed and we both vowed to watch ourselves even more carefully.

If we didn't stop too often we'd soon be in Bosquet, our point of debarkation. River travel was a risky thing at best, though, and subject to many hazards; sandbars that could ground a boat and snags that could rip out the bottom. A pilot had to be cautious of all sorts of drifting matter and sudden lows and highs in the river. Navigating the big river was never an easy thing, as the river itself was always changing and always presenting new dangers. Someday I would like to take a trip on one of these steamers, when I could relax and enjoy myself.

Gunner leaned on the gunwale and spit a stream of black tobacco juice in the waters below.

'Once we get back to Belton, Dot, what do you figure on doing?' he asked.

I pondered a moment before answering, not really sure of the answer, myself. I was a man who liked the feel of a good horse under me, and a ride out where the long wind bends the grass. I liked the sight of longhorns on the trail and hills on the horizon. I wanted to ride over the mountains and see the plains where the buffalo grazed, and walk beside streams full of trout and beaver. It was travelling I wanted to do and I said as much.

'It has a pretty sound to it, Dot, the way you tell it. I've a hankering to ride along with you when you go.'

'You're welcome, then,' I said, 'but first we've got to get this gold back to Texas.'

The river rolled past the hull and the whispering it made was soothing. The deck below was piled high with cargo heading down river to New Orleans. Gunner said he had seen these boats piled so high with bales of cotton that even at midday folks had to light candles to see.

Evening came and with it, mosquitoes. Not a lot, but enough to be known. Where the river was wide they were few, but closer to shore their numbers increased.

Gunner had retired and I stood alone on the deck, lost in my own thoughts. It was funny how a man got caught up in his own life. His own hopes and dreams. To most, only the things that directly affected their lives were of importance, but as the vastness of this land and this river passed me by, I realized how big a world we lived in. It was in me to make my mark upon the land some day, and it was big things I wanted to see and do. If only young in years, I was a man grown, and the whole of the world lay before me.

Each man born into this land has the chance of opportunity. The chance to become as big as his ambitions could make him. What a man did and what a man became ultimately depended on how much he wanted and how hard he tried. I've heard it told that the young want everything and that was a fact with me, only the ways and means by which to attain such high aspirations had not yet made themselves clear to me. But they would in time. In time they would, or so I believed.

The sound of feet came on the deck behind me and instinctively I ducked, half-turning to face the noise. A body hit me, and the hiss of a knife blade whistled past my ear.

My ducking caused the body to fall across me and I thrust upward with my legs and arms, heaving the body out and over the railing. He fell a long ways, as we were a good piece above the water and when he hit, it was with a loud splash. After a moment he came up, thrashing and spluttering about in the water.

It was him again, the man from the stables.

'How's the water, friend?' I asked. 'A might late for a swim, isn't it?'

He answered, but his answer was almighty unpleasant. Strange how some folks could get so upset about taking a bath.

When we tied up at Bosquet, I was the first down the gang-plank. Slim and Gunner were close behind as we made our way up the street to town.

This little town on a bend of the Mississippi was an on-and-off point for travellers and traders. Along the dock, shipments stood ready for loading, and already hands were offloading cargo from the steamer, making room for the next load.

We left this sight behind us, three roughly dressed men toting our gear and saddles over our shoulders with six-guns strapped to our sides.

We purchased horses easily and wasting no time in town, we hit the trail. Plush was the land we rode over and our horses stepped out nicely. It was a good day to ride and ride we did. The closer we got to Texas, the faster I wanted to travel; like a tired horse quickens its step the nearer it gets to its barn.

Three days later, we came to Alexandria and she lay spread out on the southern bank of the Red River. Lodgepole pine provided shade, and a more peaceful city I had never seen.

This, too, was a trading town, and cotton, corn and sacks of sugar lined the boardwalks as we rode by. Some Cajuns passed us, speaking their poetic language that I liked so much but could neither make heads nor tails out of.

We bought supplies in a country store, a little store that smelled of everything in it. Rich, wonderful smells of fresh-ground coffee, cured hams and bacon, new leather, spices and gun oil. The people were friendly and smiled as they filled our order.

We bought bacon, coffee, dried fruit, flour and even peaches in a can. After our order was filled, Slim Hite and Gunner Walls loaded our purchases and moved up the street to the hotel. I stayed behind looking over a new rifle the store owner brought out.

It was then that she came in. Tall and slim with dark hair and the biggest, brownest eyes I had ever seen. She moved with the grace of the finest ladies and when her eyes met mine, a smile came quickly to her face. I nodded as she passed me and spoke to the storekeeper.

'Are you Mr Stringfellow?'

'That I am, miss. May I help you with something?'

'I was told to see you about finding a guide who could escort me to Natchitoches. The two men I had previously hired left me here and I find myself stranded.'

She looked around at me, a nervous look in her eyes. From her attire, I would guess her to be a big city lady, perhaps in Alexandria on some business or such. She was young, too, I would say no more than twenty, and I pitied her being stranded in a town like this.

'I know of no one who is headed upriver,' the storekeeper said. 'But you might be able to hire a boat down at the docks.'

'That horrid place? And the men, they are so . . . rude, shall I say? No, thank you,' she went on, looking back at me. 'I prefer to go by horse.' She looked anxiously at the store-keeper and went on, 'I can pay, too, and pay well. Surely

37

someone in town would help? I'm afraid of being here alone.'

She had a frightened look on her face. I could understand that, being such a pretty, naïve young woman. With her looks, she would be subject to the advances of any man with at least one eye in his head. Alexandria, too, was a town full of questionable characters along the docks and the shacks near the river. A woman of such gentle qualities would be like a sheep among wolves.

'Miss,' I interrupted, 'how soon must you be in Natchitoches?'

She turned a hopeful look at me and answered, 'I must be there within a few days. My brother is to meet me. My aunt is very sick and not expected to live much longer. I want to be close to her during her last days. Are you going that way?'

'Not exactly, but it's not too far off course.'

'Then may I hire you to escort me?'

'No, ma'am,' I said. 'You can't hire me, or us I should say, but my partners and I may see you to Natchitoches as a kindness. We are traveling fast, though. When could you be ready to ride?'

'Why, right now, I suppose,' she answered happily. 'I have only my trunk to retrieve.'

I turned to the storekeep and asked of him, 'Where might a person purchase a horse in town?'

Before he could answer, the young woman said, 'There's no need for that. I have two outside of town. A packhorse and the one I was riding. There were two others, but the men I had employed absconded with them.'

I looked at her clothing; a beautiful green-colored dress with lace and an off-colored sash tied around her waist with a bow above the bustle in back. She wore a hat with a yellow ribbon around it and a plume of snowy white egret feathers on the side. She could never ride like this and I said as much.

'If you'll only allow me a moment, I'll change into suitable clothing. I have a room at the hotel across the street.'

I returned the Winchester to the storekeeper and readied to leave.

'Oh, I don't even know your name?' she said, by way of question.

'Dot Pickett, ma'am,' I said, removing my hat, 'from Washington, Texas.'

She offered her hand to me and I took it gently, not wanting to crush her dainty fingers.

'I'm Antoinette Thibodeaux,' she said sweetly, her brown eyes looking straight into mine. 'From St Louis.' She curtsied then, the first time anyone had ever done so to me and I found myself embarrassed. Why, I didn't know, but she seemed not to notice. Least ways, I hoped not.

CHAPTER FIVE

We left the store together and I accompanied her across the street to the hotel; the same hotel where Slim and Gunner now waited. They were lounging about in the lobby when we came in and at the sight of us, their mouths dropped open big enough to swallow apples. I knew how they felt, as this girl was a looker. Knock me dead with a skillet if she weren't!

I held my head high – proud, I suppose, at being with such a lady. They continued to stare as we walked by, their eyes following us to the desk.

Miss Thibodeaux left for her room and I walked over to the men. They were paying me no never mind, their eyes still on the young lady who was quickly disappearing up the stairs.

'Close your mouth, Gunner,' I said. 'You'll catch flies.'

They both faced me then, Slim asking the question.

I explained of my meeting Miss Thibodeaux and how she had been stranded in Alexandria. When I told them I had volunteered to escort her to Natchitoches, they exchanged glances, but made no comment.

Beautiful women have a way of making a man uncomfortable and I could understand that. But I had never seen a woman as beautiful as Antoinette Thibodeaux. Her company was something I was looking forward to and it wasn't until they mentioned the gold that I had second thoughts of my own.

Under the spell of her beauty, I had forgotten the gold. Helping a lady in distress was a gentlemanly thing to do, or so they say in stories about knights, dragons and 'damsels in distress'. But were trouble to come because of what we carried, she would be in the centre of it. If harm came to her, it would be my fault and I was of a mind to back out. If we left her in Alexandria, trouble could still befall her, so either way you looked at it she was in a mess. At least with us, she would have protection. And the three of us could do a lot of protecting if we had to.

Two days at most it would take to reach Natchitoches. Then she would be safe with her own. Surely we could afford her safety that long. Besides, there had been something about her eyes. Something intriguing and exciting all at once, something that made me long within myself to look into them once more.

She returned shortly and although her attire was different, she was nonetheless fetching.

A wide-brimmed hat had replaced the other and a long sleeved brown shirt was buttoned to the neck.

She wore riding pants, jodhpurs I believed they were called, and they were tucked neatly into shiny brown riding boots.

I had brought her trunk from the store for her and Gunner now took the valise she carried at her side, stumbling in his haste to do so.

Our intentions had been to stay over in Alexandria and catch a good night's rest at the hotel. A bit of good cooking would have fit the bill nicely, too, but with the lady's needs being urgent, we would forego our intended respite. It was still midday and ten miles or so we could make easily.

We walked together, Antoinette and I, as Gunner and Slim rode, the latter leading my horse.

On the outskirts of town, a farmhouse lay sprawled

among tall pines and hock-high grass, green under the sun. Her horses were there, all right; a long-legged sorrel and a roan packhorse.

I threw a diamond hitch on the roan and loaded the trunk and valise, adding some supplies from our horse to even the load.

A man I had ridden up the trail to Dodge with once had been fond of the word 'tranquil', saying it meant calm, peaceful, quiet and gentle all at once. This was the land we now rode, with Spanish moss drooping from its lofty place among the limbs of the many live oaks that grew along the banks of the Red River.

Rabbits scurried from underfoot and quail ran ahead of us, ducking in and out of the grass that blew gently in the breeze.

Gunner Walls and Slim Hite were quiet, content to leave the talking to Antoinette and me. She talked of things I knew naught, from parties and balls in St Louis to gowns and dresses from France. Her parents were well-to-do St Louisians and had promised her to the son of a prominent businessman. She had not been consulted and had not approved. When she received word that her aunt had taken to her deathbed, she had seized the opportunity to flee St Louis and her unwanted beau.

She had traveled the big river like us, only she had hired two guides in Bosquet to take her west across Louisiana to Natchitoches. They had turned out to be a sorry, drunken lot, leaving her stranded in Alexandria. Had we not come along, she could have been there for days.

The sun began to set and I looked for a good spot to camp. We found a suitable place and although Antoinette had ridden well, she was glad to stop for the day.

Gunner built a fire and prepared supper. While he did, we other three sat and talked.

'I was born outside Fort Elliott in the Texas Panhandle,' I said in answer to one of Antoinette's questions. 'My pa pulled up stakes from Missouri, moving to Texas to give ranching a go. It was a small place we had – one that would be called a rawhide outfit today.

'I remember little of those days, as I was only five when my ma and pa were killed. A marauding band of Comanches came through the Panhandle, stealing horses as they went. Pa, he tried to stop them, and Ma hid me behind the wood-pile out back.

'The shots I remember, and Ma's screaming. They killed them both, the Comanches did, and for a long time after the shots had stopped, I stayed in my hiding place, too scared to move while hoping not to be found. When I came out, I found them both in the yard, shot dead by Comanche guns.'

Across the fire, Antoinette sat unmoving, her eyes as big as saucers.

'I took a shovel and dug their graves. Two days it had taken, but before I could bury them, a patrol from Fort Elliott came by. They finished the job and, packing my belongings, I returned to the fort with them.

'I became a roustabout, doing odd jobs around the fort. When I was ten or so, some folks who had a ranch south of the Palo Duro Canyon took me in. I worked hard and learned as much as I could about cow critters and ranching, but finally them folks tired of their lonely existence and hard work under the hot Texas sun. They pulled up and left for California and I stayed behind.

'Been working on ranches from here to there ever since. I'd like to have one of my own someday, maybe in Colorado or Wyoming. That's big country I hear it told, and someday I would like to see it.'

The gurgling of the Red could be heard as she slowly flowed by. Now and then the cooing of doves roosting for the night broke the silence. Forgotten for the moment were Caxton and his men.

I felt as if I could sit here and talk to Antoinette forever, so nice was the feeling. The flickering of the fire and the clear sky full of stars smiling down at us as we sat huddled nigh the fire.

Gunner had turned in and now Slim left to do likewise. I looked across the fire at Antoinette, the dying fire casting vague shadows over her face.

'I'll fix your bedding so you can get some sleep. Daybreak will be here soon enough.'

She rose from the log she had been sitting on, stretching her aching muscles. 'Thanks, Dot, I *am* tired!'

I spread her blankets where the grass was thickest and rolled up another to place at her head for a pillow. Sitting down on the blankets, she slipped her boots off, setting them close by her side. Her hand tested the blanket beneath her, and apparently satisfied at how I had prepared her bedding, she removed her shirt, revealing some type of feminine undergarment beneath. Embarrassed, I turned away, allowing her privacy.

When she had turned in, I did the same and from my place on the ground, I could see the outline of her figure across from me. I watched for a moment. Her breathing was deep and even. She was asleep and soon, so was I.

Slim Hite woke me when dawn was just a hint on the horizon. I rose quickly, putting on my hat first and then my boots.

Gunner lay snoring and I kicked him playfully as I passed. He only grunted, but soon was up, too.

When I returned to the now-burning fire, Slim had coffee on and was slicing bacon into a pan. I poured a cup, liking the warm feel in my hand as I sat stiffly where Antoinette had earlier.

Looking over at her bedding, I saw she was about and I looked around for her. She had probably gone down to the river to wash up and my gaze returned to Slim as he prepared breakfast.

A moment later Gunner came up to the fire, a strange look on his face.

'Dot,' he said in a peculiar voice. 'Have you seen Antoinette this morning?'

'No, I haven't. She's probably down at the river washing up.'

'If she is, she took her horses with her.'

Startled, I turned to look at him. 'What do you mean by that?'

'I mean her horses are gone. Both of them.'

I rose to my feet then, knocking my coffee to the ground in my haste. Hurriedly, I moved to her bedding. It was unmade and cold to my touch. She had been up a while then, and a sense of foreboding hit me.

Quickly, we moved to the horses, checking for hers. They were gone, all right, as were her trunk and valise.

'What the hell?' I said aloud to Gunner.

He shrugged his shoulders and it was then that the thought hit me.

In a panic, I ran to my belongings and snatched out my saddle-bags. They were empty and a sinking feeling hit me right in the guts.

Again I checked, but there was no getting around it. The gold was gone, every last sack of it.

I cast about for sign and by the time the sun was full over the horizon, I had the story.

She had come in her stocking feet to the head of my bed where I slept. The gold had been there in my saddle-bags, not three feet from my head. As tired as I was, I hadn't heard her and once she removed the gold, she had placed it in her valise.

I found where it had rested on the ground as she filled it.

She had returned to her bed then, pulling on her boots and leaving the bedding unmade and un-slept in. From her movements and sureness of action, it was evident that she had known of the gold beforehand. But how? How could she have possibly known?

Oh, I had been duped; there was no gainsaying that. And duped by a beautiful girl with dark hair and big brown eyes.

She had been put on to us, that was the only answer. Somehow, Caxton Banks or those associated with him had gotten word to her ahead of us and as slick as a whistle, she had separated us from the gold.

After leaving her bedding, she had saddled her horse and led it out of camp, the packhorse in tow and now carrying our gold.

There, she had mounted up and ridden silently away, leaving us behind as we slept the night away. Four hours start she had, and even for a girl it was a big lead. The tracks had pointed back toward Alexandria and it was there I was sure she would return.

If she was in direct contact with anyone, they would be there waiting for her. Once she arrived, they could reunite and leave for St Louis, or wherever they had come from.

There was nothing I could do. I would have to follow her and get back the gold.

Sad were the faces that morning as we broke camp. It was my fault and I knew it, but neither Slim or Gunner laid blame about.

I was embarrassed, I admit, having been taken like I had. I was ashamed, too, as many folks were counting on that gold and I had let them down. All of them.

'You boys will have to go on back to Texas,' I said. 'Someone has to let the ranchers know what happened. Myself,' I said resolutely, 'I'm going after the gold.'

They both looked down at their feet, neither saying a word.

'Odds are,' I went on, 'that the gold is long gone. But even so, I must try to retrieve it.

'When you boys get back to Belton, make sure and tell the story straight. It was my doing – and none but mine – that cost us the gold. Don't try to cover for me. Lay it out straight.'

'Hell, Dot,' Slim said. 'Weren't no ways to tell something like that was going to happen. That girl taken me in as well as you and probably Gunner, too.' Gunner nodded in agreement and Slim continued.

'How a body could have ever suspected something like that is beyond me. We just ran into a stacked deck, Dot, that's all it be.'

'Maybe so, Slim, but I should have slept with that gold under my head and this wouldn't have happened.'

'Yeah, and maybe she'd have slit your throat for it, too. Don't be second-guessing yourself. What's done is done. Whyn't you let us come with you? We'll get it back. Hell, that girl can't go unnoticed. She's too much of a looker. Someone will see her and we'll come up with her soon or late.'

I thought a moment before answering, but stuck to my first feelings. 'No, you boys head back. Not that I don't want you, but someone has to let the folks know what has happened. There's no telling where this trail will go, or end. I'd do best to ride it alone. It's none of your doing no how.'

'Are you sure, Dot? We'll come if you say, and you know it.'

'I'm sure, Gunner. You boys go on. This is something I have to handle myself. You tell the folks that as long as I breathe, I'll hunt that gold and until I find it, I'll never rest. Do I come back to Texas, I'll come bringing the gold.'

CHAPTER SIX

I pushed my horse hard, as the tracks left by Antoinette were easy to follow. She had moved right along, herself, and by the time I returned to Alexandria, I had only gained an hour or so.

I checked with the hotel and storekeeper and every other place I could think of, but no one had seen her.

Next I checked the riverfront where boats were always coming and going. Not steamers or paddlewheelers, but riverboats; dugouts, canoes and keelboats.

A rough lot hung around the river and of a disposition to talk they were not, but one man did tell of a fancy dressed lady and a man who had hired a boat earlier that morning.

'They came 'round just after sunup,' he said, his old broken teeth working around a chaw of black tobacco. 'Seemed almighty in a hurry. Parkins, he took them on. Paid him well, they did, and cut the river shortly after.' He paused to spit a glob of tobacco juice on the ground, wiping his mouth with the back of his shirtsleeve. 'A mighty fine looking lass, the lady was. One of the finest I ever seen and I seen a'plenty.' The old man cackled, nodding his head up and down at some secret memories.

'What about the man with her?' I asked. 'What did he look like?'

'Oh, him? Tall man,' he said, ''bout thirty-five or so. Big hands and wide shoulders. A New Orleans fella, half French, if you ask me.'

'Did you know him?'

'Can't say's I did, but I knew his type,' he spat again and went on. 'River man, he was, probably one of those Natches-Under-The-Hill boys. A lot of robbing, killing and piracy those boys did. Funny thing, too. . . .' he stopped then and looked at me and I prodded.

'What funny thing?'

'That girl with him, she seemed to be afraid of him. It weren't like they was hitched to each other or even just friendly-like. She seemed plumb scared of the man. Struck me as kinda strange then, but I didn't get old sticking my nose where it don't belong.'

I thought about what he said. Why would she be afraid of the man with her? Were they together in this, as I suspected? Or was there something deeper to it? Had she only joined up with him once returning to Alexandria? Or had she been forced to go along?

Maybe he was the contact of Caxton and had simply used or hired Antoinette to do his bidding.

'How did she seem afraid of this man?'

From his place on an old keg, his hands carved shavings from a stick, the whittlings falling at his feet. He peered across the river as if trying to dredge up the pictures that his eyes had seen.

'Couple of times there,' he said, 'she tried to break away from his hold, as if she wanted to get away from him. Everywhere they went, he kept a tight grip on her arm, never letting her loose even once.

'When they finally hired a boat, he practically threw her in it and as they pushed off, they argued something fierce till clean out of sight.'

'Did you catch where they were going?' I asked hopefully.

'No, can't rightly say I did, but I knows. Weren't but one place that man was going and where you find him, you'll find her.' He carved a few more slivers from the stick, his toe nudging the shavings that lay covered with tobacco juice. 'No'leans, son. That's where they was going. You'll find them there if you find them a'tall.'

So here I was again, selling my horses for a ride down the river. I had always wanted to see New Orleans, but would have preferred the circumstances to be different.

Luckily, I had paid Gunner, Slim and myself out of the gold. When it was stolen, we hadn't lost everything, although that was small consolation. At least I wasn't penniless and in a city like New Orleans, a man would have to have money to get anything.

Once again, I boarded a steamer in Bosquet, this time heading south to the big city. I took a stateroom called the Texas, which I chose because of being from Texas. Mayhap not a strategic way to choose a room, but she was a nice one and the highest point on a riverboat, 'cept for the pilot-house.

It was said along the river that Henry M. Shreve, a trader and steamboat builder for whom Shreveport was named, had given the cabins on the riverboats the names of various states. Thereafter, folks had taken to calling them state-rooms.

As I sat in my stateroom, I wondered what had become of the man who had jumped me up the river and had taken a swim for his troubles. Was he acting, as I had first thought, on the behalf of the stable owner? Or was he under the orders of Caxton Banks?

The man who had joined with Antoinette in Alexandria hadn't been he, as the description was wrong, so there were at least three people in the state of Louisiana who had been involved in an attempt to take the gold, with the last being successful.

Who were all of these people? Were they all united through a common factor and if so, was that factor Caxton Banks? If he was, then where was he? Still on the Chisholm looking for us? Or was he now in Louisiana as well?

Telegrams and cables could be sent, which would explain the contacting of people downriver and ahead of us. But men couldn't travel by telegram or cable, so Caxton and his group had to be behind me somewhere.

Would he go on to New Orleans to join with those who now had the gold? Or had Antoinette and the man with her acted independently and stolen the gold on their own? If so, there were now three factions involved, each wanting the gold and each prepared to kill for it, including myself.

Who was the man with Antoinette? From her actions, she had not been desirous of his company, or at least was unpleased with something that had transpired.

Where did all of these pieces fit? Where did it all come together? Why had Antoinette betrayed our trust, other than the financial rewards? Had she been paid to do so or had she found out about the gold on her own? Was she involved with Caxton in some way? I found that hard to believe, although there were confidence people who were like actors when it came to playing a role designed to separate a party from their valuables.

There were a lot of questions that needed answers and I had a feeling that those answers would be found in New Orleans. The only concern I had was that in seeking these answers and in ultimately trying to recover the gold, a man would run into those trying to stop him. The method of doing so would be no secret. It would be death, quick and sure.

I debarked at Baton Rouge for a two-hour layover. One of the men on the steamer was from Baton Rouge and he said the name of the city was from the French language meaning 'Red Stick'. I didn't see any red sticks about, but there may have been some back then.

Up the street I found a place to get a drink. I had never been to Baton Rouge before, but bars were plenty and easy to find. The one I entered was called 'Brown's Hole'. It was a small place and only a few people sat around drinking.

I asked the barkeep if he had seen a tall man with a beautiful woman. He said he hadn't and I left it at that, as I doubted they would even bother to get off here when they could stay on the boat in comfort.

The man behind the bar was a friendly sort and I passed the time yarning with him. Seems he had been around in his days, having sailed on the big ships. He lost a leg during a squall and had retired to shore, running this little bar on the north side of Baton Rouge.

He poured me another drink and moved on down the bar, humming an Irish ditty as he went. It was then they came in, three men off the street, and naturally I turned to look as they entered.

When I saw them, I knew trouble was at hand. A man who's tasted trouble over and over after a while gets to where he can sense its presence long before it shows itself. I knew these men were looking for trouble and that trouble would end with me.

There was a lot of killing and shooting that went on along the river and a different lot they were from gunmen. These men were big and almighty mean looking, but mostly they did their fighting or killing in a bunch with clubs, fists, knives and anything they could lay their hands on. Although they were dangerous enough, they were not gunmen.

I turned to the barkeep, who had returned, and spoke

out of the corner of my mouth, 'You'd best move down the way, mister. This here is going to be a shooting.'

He looked at them, then back to me, and quickly moved to the far end of the bar.

One of the men before me appeared to be the leader of the bunch. He had a scraggly mustache and broken, yellow teeth. The brim of his hat was broken and hung down over his forehead.

The two men with him shifted, one to the left and one to the right.

'OK, cowboy,' the leader said, 'you've got yourself a choice. You can die where you stand, or you can go back where you came from. We know why you're here and we know what you're after.' He leaned forward then and whispered where only I could hear. 'The lady is gone, cowboy. There's nothing here for you.'

'What lady?' I asked innocently. 'I know nothing of any lady.'

I said it loud and the men in the bar turned to look, each staring at the men huddled before me. The leader looked around nervously, eyeing the others in the room.

'Don't play dumb, cowboy. We know the score and so do you. Just hitch your belt up and head back to cow country. If you do, there won't be any trouble.'

'Trouble?' I asked, as if surprised. 'Why, I was raised on trouble. What kind of trouble might you mean?'

'Gun trouble!' the man said angrily. 'Now just get on out of here.'

These men had come prepared for violence and a killing, and given the chance they would do just that. Probably hired by the man with Antoinette, or possibly even Antoinette herself, as a precaution against any of us trailing them and trying to recover the gold. They had been instructed to run any of us out of town or kill us if we refused.

53

Being as only one man had come, they were confident of their ability to carry out their orders. Not being gunmen, they were not aware of just what a man fast with a gun could do. They figured their numbers enough to run me out of town and at three to one, they didn't expect anyone but a fool to reach for a gun. And no one but a fool would. A fool, or a man fast with a gun.

I had always been fast and a dead shot, too. These men had come to harm or kill, and being so, they knew the risk. Mercy I would not show, as they would not know the meaning of it.

I drew and fired, quicker than anyone could think. My bullet took the leader in the face and he fell back screaming, clawing at his wound as he hit the floor.

The man to the left reached frantically for his gun as I turned and cut loose at him.

The third man had raised his hands and now he was stumbling backwards, a look of pure horror on his face.

These men were sure-thing killers, not fighters, and the suddenness with which death had come threw them into shock.

The man with his hands up said pleadingly, 'Don't shoot, mister. For the Lord's sake, don't shoot!'

I held my gun ready, looking from one to the other. The leader lay on the floor, sobbing into hands that covered his bleeding face. The other man lay dead, a neat bullet hole in the centre of his head.

'All right,' I said. 'Put your hands down and see to your friend.'

'Want me to drop my gun?' he asked frightfully.

'No, sir! You get a hankering to draw, you go right ahead.'

Nervously, he kept his hands far from his gun as he bent down to help his partner. The man on the floor had quit sobbing and his hands had grown still.

'Too late,' I said. 'He's dead. Take him out and bury him along with the other. You started this mess, now you can clean it up.'

Slowly, he dragged one and then the other body out of the bar. A crowd had gathered out front and they watched silently.

As the last body was hauled outside, the survivor rose, wiping his bloody hands on his pant leg.

'Who put you up to this?' I asked. 'Who gave you this job?'

He thought about lying, I could see it. But the sight of my gun still pointed at him changed his mind.

'A lady,' he said. 'A fancy lady down at the river.'

I motioned with my gun for him to continue and he went on.

'We each got a hundred dollars and in gold. She said the job would be easy. Just some cowboy from cow country.'

'And what was her name?' I prodded.

'Antoinette,' he answered. 'Antoinette Thibodeaux.'

'Was there anyone with her?'

'Yes,' he answered, looking down at his feet gloomily.

'Well, who was he?'

'He'll kill me if I tell you. Let me leave, mister. I just want to get out of here.'

'If you don't tell me his name, you'll be joining your friends.'

I earred back the hammer of my pistol and he spit out the name, 'André Bontemps! It was he that was with her.'

'And how did you come to know him?'

'Jake and Sam,' he said, nodding at his two dead companions. 'We pulled jobs for him here and there. In New Orleans, mostly.'

'And what about the lady with him? Had you met her before?'

'Yes, in New Orleans. She and André are always together. It was she that paid us, not André. I think she wanted it kept secret from him.' He paused and looked up from his feet to stare at me. 'Who are you, mister? What are you doing chasing after Miss Antoinette?'

I only looked at him, ignoring his question.

'He will kill you,' he said, half-gloating. 'André will kill you. He'll stand for no one bothering Miss Antoinette. He is a dangerous man. Even you with your gun tricks, you won't have a chance with him.'

I had never heard of this man André Bontemps, but at least now I had his name. If he were to return to New Orleans, he would now be a lot easier to find. At least I had that to work on.

'What do I do now?' the man asked, looking at the bodies that lay in the street.

'See that they are buried and then get out of town. You ever see a lynching?' I finished.

He shook his head fearfully, looking around at the faces in the crowd.

'Then I suggest you get moving.'

CHAPTER SEVEN

New Orleans was quite the city. Everything I had expected and more. I felt out of place in my shabby trail clothes and I drew more than a few glances as I walked down the street.

I wandered about most of the morning, seeing the sights and trying to come up with some sort of plan. New Orleans was much bigger than I had believed and finding Antoinette and André Bontemps might turn out to be a bigger task than I had at first anticipated. Were a person mindful of losing oneself, they could surely do so in New Orleans.

As I followed the narrow, winding streets that wove in and about the city, I came to the Vieux Carré, also known as the French Quarter. Jackson Square was in the heart of this section of New Orleans and it was there that I sat down and commenced to figuring.

You would think that finding a man like André Bontemps would be easy. New Orleans was a city of many sights and many lights. Not the kind of city that a man would want to lay low in, but the kind that would drive a man to be out and about.

André Bontemps, too, would have little reason to concern himself about me. After all, he hadn't stolen any gold and had more than likely forgotten all about me. Of course, that also depended on how much Antoinette had told him about me, if even anything. She had been the one who hired the three men in Baton Rouge. Perhaps André Bontemps knew nothing of me at all. It was this, I hoped, that would make him easier to find. And like the old man in Bosquet had said, where I found André, I would find Antoinette.

The first thing I needed was someone who knew the city and its language. Someone who was familiar with New Orleans inside and out. The city would be full of people like that, as all along the waterfront there were thieves, pick-pockets and hustlers looking to make a fast buck. From what the man in Baton Rouge had said, André Bontemps would be known to this sort of ruffians.

There were places in New Orleans, also, where a man would do best to avoid. Rough places where only the tough-est of men dared venture. I had heard of them before and from those who would know.

They were rough and tumble dives, like Billy Phillip's 101 Ranch, The Frenchman's, Lulu White's Mahogany Hall and The Five Dollar House.

On Gallatin Street, you'd find the Blue Anchor, Mother Burke's Den, The Amsterdam and The Canton House. All rough places and good places to avoid.

André Bontemps would not be found in any of these, but were I right about the man, those who knew him would. The best thing I could do would be to find someone who had access to these places, or at least to the people who gathered there.

I took a room at the Saint Charles. My attire brought a scowl from the clerk, but when I paid in gold, he brightened up.

We talked a good bit, he and I, and seems like the Bontemps name was a well-known one to him. André he didn't know, but he did know of a man who knew everyone and everything in New Orleans.

This man's name was Ring and he was a Cajun who lived along the Bayou Teche. He would be the one, he said, to help me find anyone or anything I wanted.

I bathed and shaved, and although my funds weren't long, I sent for a tailor and had a suit of clothes made. Not that I was much on fancy clothes, but in a city like New Orleans, it wouldn't be wise to walk around sticking out like a sore thumb. Not when a man was hunting another and one who wouldn't hesitate to have me killed if he knew I were here.

When my clothes came early the next morning, I put them on and they fit nicely. I must admit, I didn't mind the way they looked and it was good I felt as I sat up for breakfast in the dining room of the Saint Charles.

My thoughts returned to the Cajun named Ring. I found it a strange name for a man and it had been the only one I was given. The clerk had said Ring would be easy to find, as everyone in the Bayou Teche knew him.

It was short of noon when I was finally ushered into the back room of a waterfront store that sold all sorts of knick-knacks. The Cajuns along the way had been close-mouthed and unfriendly, but they had nonetheless pointed me in the direction of Ring.

He sat there before me now, in a smoke-filled room with just enough light to see. He was younger than I had thought, only forty or so, and the reason he was called Ring was immediately apparent.

From each ear hung large gold rings, and through his nose ran a smaller one.

His hair was dark and long, falling way below his shoulders. Around his waist ran a wide, black belt. Inside it were tucked at least six knives, the handles of various sizes and shapes.

His eyes were dark and penetrating and a mischievous

smile ran across his face.

In the room with him were men dressed akin to him, only missing the golden rings. They each stared at me, expressionless; all but the man called Ring.

'What may I do for you?' he finally asked, speaking in a deep, Cajun accent.

'I am looking for a man, and a woman, too,' I answered. 'I've been told you could help me find them.'

He looked at the others around him and then back to me.

'There are many men and women in New Orleans. Why do you look for these two?'

I hesitated, knowing that to mention the gold would be unwise. 'They have something of mine. Something I wish to recover.'

He laughed then, Ring did, and looked at me curiously. 'Could it be the man has the woman that belongs to you?'

I hesitated again before answering, thinking maybe it best to let his thoughts run in this direction.

'Let's just say that the woman was with me, then she was gone. When next she was seen, she was in the company of the gentleman I seek.'

Ring cast a knowing glance at his companions, but somehow I believed he sensed there was a deeper reason for my seeking the man and woman.

'There isn't much in New Orleans that I don't know,' he finally said, waving his hands in a motion that seemed to encompass all about him. 'Who is the man you seek?'

'André Bontemps.'

His eyes widened and he whistled in surprise.

'Aw, André,' he said, shaking his head. 'I know him well. And would the woman you seek be Antoinette Thibodeaux?'

Now it was my turn to be surprised and it must have shown on my face.

'Yes,' Ring said, 'I know everything worth knowing in New

Orleans. I take it by your expression that I am right.'

'That you are,' I answered. 'Antoinette Thibodeaux is the woman I wish to find.'

He motioned for me to join him at the table and when I had, he pushed a bottle of rum and a cup my way.

As I poured myself a drink, he sat still, obviously deep in thought. But finally he spoke.

'Bontemps is a well-known name in New Orleans and in all of Louisiana, for that matter. André, he is the son of Philippe Bontemps, who owns the Sabre Plantation just out of the city. He is well-to-do and very much so, owning four or five sugar plantations, many warehouses in New Orleans and half a dozen ships that sail out of the gulf. The Bontemps have been in New Orleans most ever since she was first founded, and a fine family they are.'

He paused to take a sip of his rum and I asked, 'And what of André? What is his position with this family?'

Ring rolled the amber liquid back and forth in his cup before answering.

'André is, shall we say, an outcast from the family. Many years ago, at least ten, André was implicated in the death of a young girl. A girl from a good family, but not rich like the Bontemps.

'Philippe,' Ring went on, 'in order to save the family name, used his money and power to bail his son out of the sticky situation. After having done so, he booted André out of his home, telling him to never return.

'André was disinherited and, no longer able to live in the manner he had become accustomed to, he turned criminal. At first he targeted his father's business, stealing loads of cotton and sugar from his warehouses and selling them to those not particular as to rightful ownership. One thing led to another and André is now involved in most of the shady dealings that occur along the waterfront.'

'And what of Antoinette?' I asked. 'What has she to do with this?'

Once again, he took a sip of his rum, this time emptying the cup. He refilled it, offering me more and I shook my head.

'Antoinette is André's mistress. They live together on the Hilliard Plantation.'

I was surprised, I admit, as Antoinette had struck me as naïve and innocent. Obviously, I had been wrong, as was proven by the gold. But to be the mistress of a crook was something I would not have believed. Yet, if a man ever seemed to be in the know, it was this man Ring.

'Can you take me to the Hilliard Plantation?' I asked.

'Most assuredly,' he replied, the smile still etched on his face.

'How much do you want?' I asked. 'What will you charge for this service?'

He rose from his seat, waving a casual hand. 'For now, nothing, my friend. I will do this as a courtesy. A favour from one man to another.'

I'll bet, I thought to myself, as I believed Ring smelled something in this. Just exactly what, he didn't know, but if I read him right, he wanted to be around when it came to light.

Two tall horses we rode, long in the leg and deep in the chest. Ring had produced them and fine enough mounts they were.

We rode for an hour and finally came to a winding drive that wove its way among hundred-year-old trees. These at last ended in a half-circle drive in front of a two-storied house with huge oaken doors.

A balcony stretched across the face of the house, supported by eight freshly-painted white columns. Wrought iron barred the windows, their shape artistically crafted in twists and swirls.

The lawn was richly green and stretched neatly all the way to the edge of the bayou. Spanish moss hung lazily from the huge old oaks, and spotted over the whole of the yard were brightly coloured flowers; azaleas and camellias and three or four others that I didn't know.

As we approached, a groom took our horses and at the door we were met by a butler in a stiff outfit of black, with a small cap on his head.

I had heard of setups like this before, but had never seen them.

Ring told the butler his name and he seemed to recognize it. Disappearing behind the door, he left us standing outside, both of us armed if the case need be.

I was unsure as to how Bontemps would react at finding me on his doorsteps. He would not know my face, but he would know the name. Although it was Antoinette who had taken the gold and she who had hired the would-be killers in Baton Rouge, had André been in on the whole thing?

For some strange reason, I felt that he hadn't, as from the looks of this plantation, Bontemps, even though estranged from his family, had become a man of means. Thirty thousand dollars in gold was a lot of money to a lot of people, but not necessarily so to those like the Bontemps. If he were, in fact, involved in crime as Ring had said, there would be easier and safer ways to make thirty thousand dollars than to traipse halfway across Louisiana to steal it from some cowhands he didn't even know. On top of that, a man like André Bontemps wouldn't have to go on such a mission. There were plenty who would gladly do it for him.

No, I didn't believe Bontemps to be a party in this, yet as Antoinette was his mistress – as Ring had said – André would take whatever steps necessary to protect her.

Interrupting my train of thought, Andre Bontemps appeared at the door. He was indeed a tall man, with dark, curly hair and a scar over his left eye that wound around the side of his head and disappeared in his hair.

A drooping mustache and another scar on his chin gave the man a sinister look, one that had an all-too-real air of danger about it.

The gaze he focused on Ring was hard, and were I not mistaken, tinged with a touch of anger.

Ring's hand rested on the butt of his pistol, while his other hovered near the cluster of knives in his belt. It was apparent that these two had met before and had not parted on good terms.

'What brings you here, Ring?' André asked angrily. He was obviously not pleased at our presence and with an effort was keeping his anger under rein.

On Ring's face was still his habitual smile, one that, in this instance, seemed to be taunting. I had a feeling that when that smile disappeared, if it ever did, that death would be shortly behind.

He stood that way a moment before answering, staring back at André belligerently.

'I bring one who wishes to see you, André,' he said, motioning to me. 'One who has business with you and the lady.'

He turned and looked at me then and his eyes were hard and cold.

I still wore the suit I had bought in New Orleans, but the jacket was open in front, the right side pushed to the back and revealing the buckled gun belt and well-used revolver. Like Ring, my hand was close to the butt of my pistol.

André turned back to Ring and with a nod of his head toward me, he asked, 'Who is he and why did you bring him here?'

Before Ring could answer, I interrupted.

'If it's me you inquire about, Monsieur Bontemps, you do so to me. I need no one to speak for me.'

A look of impatience crossed his face and he turned his look to me once again.

'All right, then, what do you wish to see me about?'

I stepped forward a few paces, leaving Ring behind me and to my right.

'It is a question of property and ownership,' I said. 'The property is mine, and the ownership is yours.'

He looked at me questioningly without reply and I went on.

'Some property of mine was separated from me outside of Alexandria. The person who did this separating was Antoinette Thibodeaux. She was in your company shortly after and returned to New Orleans with you.'

'Are you claiming that Antoinette has taken something from you?'

'That I am, and I have come to reclaim it.'

His face turned angry again and he said hotly, 'I know nothing of your property or of your dealings with Antoinette. What may have transpired between you and her is of no concern to me now.'

'You made it your concern when you brought Antoinette back to New Orleans with you. If you had nothing to do with the three men in Baton Rouge, then surely you must have had some knowledge of it.'

'Aw, so you are the one?' he asked, a look of understanding crossing his face. 'Antoinette said you seemed to be a persistent one. I see she was right.'

Ring stood quietly where he was, saying nothing but taking in every word with keen interest.

'I am here for my property, Mr Bontemps, and I have no time to shilly-shally around. Your association with Miss

Thibodeaux is no concern to me. The only matter of importance is the return of my property. I strongly suggest to you, sir, that it be returned, and returned immediately.'

Bontemps came down the steps and stood before me not six feet away. His face had turned red and the veins on his temple stood out.

'Who do you think you are,' he practically shouted, 'coming to my home and threatening me? I know nothing of your property, only that you attempted to persuade Antoinette to leave Louisiana with you. When she refused, you held her against her will and had she not escaped you in the night, there is no telling what would have happened to her.'

I stood there, shocked by his words. Such a distortion of the truth I had never heard. The story was so far from the facts that it was ludicrous. Whoever had told him this tale had obviously made him believe it.

'I am afraid that you have been misinformed, Mr Bontemps. No such thing happened, nor anything even close to it. Miss Thibodeaux approached me in Alexandria requesting an escort to Natchitoches so she could be with her dying aunt. I, and two men with me, agreed to see her safely to her destination. Late in the night, however, she left us, absconding with the property I now seek.'

He looked at me disbelieving, and I knew that whoever had told him this tale had convinced him beyond a doubt. Only Antoinette could have related this story to him and she had done so well. Still, the truth had been stretched and I had gold to recover. Were André foolish enough to believe such a story, then he would have to pay for his folly. I had no intention of mollycoddling a man who had been taken in by his mistress. That gold I must recover and did he stand in my way, I would lay him with the others.

'Your story is, at most, inaccurate,' André Bontemps said.

'But I shall give you a chance to refute what Antoinette has told me, in person.'

With that, he turned and called over his shoulder. A moment later, the clicking of heels sounded from inside to be followed by the appearance of Antoinette Thibodeaux at the doorway. She descended the steps carefully to join André, standing innocently by his side. The face she turned to him was the one I had seen in the store back in Alexandria, all innocent and naïve.

'Is this the man you told me of?' André asked of her. 'Is he the one who held you against your will?'

Antoinette looked at me, a picture of innocence had I ever seen one. When she was satisfied, she turned back to him, answering primly, 'Yes, André, he is the one. What is he doing here?'

'Never mind what he's doing here, he hasn't much longer to stay.'

'Hold on, there,' I interrupted. 'This has gone far enough. I never held anyone against their will and I never would.' Ignoring André, I turned to Antoinette and asked, 'Where is my property? The property you stole while we lay asleep. What you stole was not mine,' I said, 'but belonged to people who are needful of it.'

She couldn't meet my eyes and quickly turned to André.

'I know nothing of any property,' she said. 'I have no idea what he is talking about. Please, André, make him go away. He frightens me!'

André stepped forward, placing himself between Antoinette and me. 'You heard what she said. Turn around now and be out of here. Whatever you are trying to do, it won't work.'

Ring had moved up to my right and now stood beside me, his shoulder brushing momentarily against mine.

'I will not leave without recovering what I have come for.

67

Return it now and I will forget the matter.'

'You have been told once, Mr Pickett. Antoinette knows nothing of your property, nor does she have any of your property.'

'Then she lies!' I yelled, the frustration and anger finally rising in me. Ring nudged me with his elbow, but I ignored him. 'For the last time, Bontemps, I will not leave until I have recovered my property, and all of it.'

At that, the anger left his face and his body relaxed. An air of confidence came over him and he said, 'So be it, then. I see we have reached an impasse. One that I am afraid must be settled, and settled on the field of honour,' he finished triumphantly.

I turned to Ring, not sure what Andre Bontemps meant by the 'field of honour'.

'It means you have been challenged,' Ring said. 'Challenged to a duel.'

I turned to André then, my anger finally getting the best of me. My right hand rose quickly and my fist landed squarely on his nose, knocking him backward where he sprawled upon the ground.

'Tell him that means I accept,' I told Ring, 'and I accept most happily.'

CHAPTER EIGHT

Just exactly what a duel entailed I couldn't say. But Ring – he knew all about them, as did André Bontemps.

We returned to the Bayou Teche and the little store where I had first met Ring. When it was told I had been challenged to a duel by André Bontemps and had accepted, the unfriendly, stoic men who had been there before became excited and vociferous.

They talked back and forth in their Cajun tongue, now and then one of them turning to look at me as if to size me up. It seemed as if dueling was a big thing to these people and they appeared to be looking forward to it anxiously.

I would need a second, Ring said, and he went on to explain, 'Being the challenged party, you have the choice of weapons; pistols or sabres. I would advise the pistols, as André is one of the finest swordsmen in all of Louisiana.'

I knew exactly what I would choose, as a sabre was something I had never seen, let alone used.

Ring said pistols would be fine and that duelling pistols would be provided. I would have preferred the use of the pistol I now carried, but any kind of pistol would suit me. I had never met anyone who could out-shoot me with any type of firearm, so what we used made no difference to me at all.

Myself, I thought the whole thing to be a bother. But if

André was going to stand in the way of my recovering the gold, then he would have to be moved aside. He had had the opportunity to do so of his own volition, but he had chosen not to. Now he would be moved aside forcibly.

Later that day a man arrived from the Hilliard Plantation. He was André's second and he and Ring went over the particulars. Seems that dueling had long since been outlawed by the government, but still, in secret places, men met to settle matters of honour.

I didn't necessarily consider this a matter of honour; merely a matter of necessity, as André stood between myself and the gold I had been entrusted with. Did I have to step over his body to recover it, I would, but I found it no matter of honor. More so a matter of business.

From what Ring said, Bontemps had earned himself quite a reputation as a duelist. Seems he had killed more than a few men, both with the sword and the pistol. The scars that I had seen on his face had been put there by the men he had met in these duels.

André, too, Ring went on to say, was not considered a traditionalist when it came to dueling. Usually, the drawing of blood was enough to satisfy one's honour, but not to André. He fought to kill and kill he had, many times.

I believed Ring when he said this, as in the man I had sensed an underlying current of anger and cruelty. I was not familiar with the exact details of André's alleged killing of the young girl, but did know that he had been shunned from the family.

This insult to his dignity and pride would be a seed of anger to lie fermenting in his belly. As time went on and the anger festered inside, it would eat away at him more and more.

It was this type of circumstance that, not only in André but in other men as well, caused a man to become hateful and cruel. It was then only understandable that the joining of these forces would bring a man to kill, and to kill again and again. It was only through this killing that the rage which burned inside could be appeased, even if only temporarily.

I had killed and I'm sure I would do so again, but never had I done so except to protect my own life, property or the lives of others.

The West these days was a wild and lawless land and one must do what one must do to survive. But there was killing and then there was murder, and not so fine a line as one might think between the two.

If I had to kill to survive, I would, as it had been this way for men throughout the ages. To kill, though, when to do so was not necessary or righteous, was to commit murder, and this I could not condone.

Ring and Bontemps' second agreed on terms: The duel would be in the morning of the following day. We would meet at a secret place in the bayous and Ring and a few of his men would go with us.

I was not nervous, which Ring found strange. Guns had been a way of life to me since I could remember. This duel was simply something that must be done, and the sooner the better. It was the gold that hung most heavily on my mind and I worried about it being moved from the plantation, if it were indeed there. Ring still did not know that it was gold I was after, but I had my suspicions that he suspected something of more than normal value. I discussed the matter with him without mentioning gold, and he agreed to have his men watch the plantation.

The next day, Ring and I went over the particulars of the duel. Each man would be given a pistol. A pair of single-shot dueling pistols would be used. André Bontemps, Ring said, was more proud of this set of dueling pistols than any of his other possessions. They were said to be the very pistols that Andrew Jackson and Charles Dickinson had used in their famous duel. Charles Dickinson was killed and Andrew Jackson went on to become the President of the United States.

After the pistols were checked and given to each man, we would stand facing each other, with the chief steward between us. At his direction, we would turn and take six paces in opposite directions before turning to fire at his command. Usually, this would end the duel, regardless of the results, but none of André's duels had ended so regimentally. On the few times that the first volley had failed to produce the death of a dueller, the pistols had been reloaded and the procedure repeated until death, or until one or the other was so seriously wounded that he could not continue.

'Speed is not necessarily the most essential thing,' Ring said, as he paced back and forth in front of me. 'All of the men who have faced André have been in such fear of his reputation that in their haste to get off the first shot, they missed. This had been true in almost every case. After missing, they were then at the mercy of Bontemps, and as I've said before, he has no mercy.'

Ring stopped his pacing to stand directly in front of me. His face was serious and his finger pointed at me to emphasize his words.

'Remember, Monsieur Pickett, speed is fine, but accuracy is final!'

The rest of the day we spent around Ring's store. Many men came in and out, most looking disreputable at best. They were a dangerous, cutthroat-looking lot, and the thought crossed my mind that in recovering the gold, André

Bontemps may turn out to be the least of my troubles. If there was a man among these who wouldn't sell his soul to the devil, I would be surprised.

Ring woke me early the next morning. It was still dark, but a hint of the rising sun peaked over the horizon. His mood was serious and gloomy, and he went about preparing breakfast and coffee in a brusque manner.

Myself, I felt refreshed and ready for whatever lay at hand. The thought of battle made my blood quicken and my heart beat rapidly. I was anxious to be on with it and when Ring's men began to drift in, a restlessness came upon me.

We ate quickly, Ring's men avoiding my eyes, apparently afraid of jinxing me. The thought brought a smile to my face, as men were a superstitious lot. I laughed out loud, a sudden, heartfelt laugh that rang loudly. The Cajuns jumped, startled, each looking away nervously, thinking that this white man had lost his wits. Jinxes, hexes and superstitions would play no role in today's events; only courage, accuracy and a will of steel. Fate, mayhap, as I did believe in fate, but I felt that if anyone was destined to go on, it was me. The world was a big place and I still had many things to do and see.

Counting myself, there were six of us who loaded aboard two worn-out old boats, three of us in each. Ring and I rode in the forward boat, one of his men in the stern behind, dipping his oar into the dark, murky waters of the bayou and propelling us forward with an easy, sure motion.

The thick canopy of trees with their clusters of Spanish moss provided a darkness that was both sobering and eerie. Overhead an egret gave its cry across the water and somewhere up ahead, an answering call drifted back to us.

The beady eyes of 'gators could be seen just above the level of water. As we grew nearer, they blinked off, disappearing with a gentle swoosh below the surface.

Bullfrogs, 'gators and night hunting owls cast their calls across the bayou as we wove our way among the cypress knees that rose from the water at the feet of their parent tree. The bayous were a strange, somewhat spooky place, yet I found myself liking this wild, lonely refuge. It was, in fact, the perfect place for a duel to the death.

The Cajuns, or at least a good many of them, made the bayous their home. They knew the subtle twists and turns of the shallow channels that dissected the waterways and where most would have made slow travel through here, we moved briskly along.

At last we came to a rise of land on which a small clearing unfolded. Two other boats were tied to cypress knees and in the clearing itself, men stood staring as we approached, their looks cold and hard, yet not hostile.

Planks had been laid from the bank into the water, the ends extending to the bottom only a foot beneath the water. We tied up to the left of these planks, across from the boats of the Bontemps party. Ring was the first to step out, and nimbly he made his way up the planks and on to the shore. I followed him and in single file behind me came the Cajuns who were Ring's men.

Bontemps stood in the centre of the clearing. His hands rested upon his hips and his feet were spread wide. Around his neck a long, silken scarf blew to and fro in the wind, whipping back and forth around his head. His shirt was unbuttoned to the waist and his pants were black and tight, their lengths disappearing into calf-high riding boots that were immaculately polished.

He was a striking figure, I'll give him that, and I believed that on seeing him standing there, most would have had second thoughts about dueling with the man. But I did not find it so. After all, he was only a man, like me, and like all men he was not infallible. He could die as well as the next and well he knew it, but he was betting on one thing: his skill and experience as a duellist.

Me, I was doing no betting. I was not here for sport or for entertainment. I was here to carry out a task and that task was to remove the man before me from the path he barred to the gold. Did that take extreme measures, then so be it. I had been left no choice in the matter.

Antoinette was absent, as I had expected, and only men were about. One of these – a tall, sallow-faced man dressed in drab clothing – spread a cloth upon the ground. Next, from a box at his feet, he removed a smaller, ornately carved box and set it in the centre of the cloth.

Ring motioned to me and together we moved to the man who now knelt on the ground in front of the box.

Inside were two pistols such as I had never seen before. They were huge guns, their bores the biggest I had ever seen. They were in excellent condition, and if pistols could ever appear savage, these did. I could see why André treasured their possession.

Bontemps stood arrogantly across from us, as his second and mine watched the loading of the pistols. These pistols were muzzle-loaders and the sallow-faced man poured a measure of powder into the muzzle of each. Then he took a ball wrapped in a patch and with a ramming rod, pushed each into the barrels of the pistols until they rested against the powder. The man's motions were slow but sure, allowing both parties to observe each step of the loading procedures.

He looked at Ring and then Bontemps' second, and when both men nodded, he continued.

Setting the ramming rod aside, he cocked both pistols and placed primer caps on the nipples. When they were in place and the man satisfied, he once again placed the two pistols on the cloth in front of us.

'The choice belongs to you, Monsieur Pickett,' the man

who was André's second said, his hands sweeping towards the pistols in a beckoning manner.

'Either will do,' I said, but when I reached for the pistol nearest me, Ring's hand shot out warding mine away, and took up the pistol I had intended.

Out of the corner of his mouth he whispered, 'A matter of etiquette.'

André Bontemps' second followed suit, possessing his pistol for him, and together we all stepped away from the cloth and loading tools that lay upon it.

The sallow-faced man, whom I deduced to be in charge of the procedure, motioned us even further back until we were almost dead centre in the clearing. There André and I stood, both truculent and ungiving, a scant two feet apart. Our seconds were to our right, both holding the pistols, and our eyes were locked on each other, like two pugilists attempting to stare the other down.

The sallow-faced man spoke.

'When I give the signal, both of you will turn with your backs to each other. You will then proceed to take six paces away from each other in a slow manner. Once you have taken the required six paces, you will both stop, holding your position as is. I will then, without undo warning, give the command to turn and fire. You may then, and only then, turn your gun upon your opponent and fire at will.'

Out of the corner of my eye, I could see Ring and Andre's second standing a short distance away, both holding revolvers in their hands. Ring had told me earlier that this would happen. If ever a dueller attempted, or in fact did fire early or in violation of the agreed-upon terms, he would instantly be shot down by both seconds.

Scattered in a rough group near me were the Cajuns, and near André Bontemps were the men with him. All were quiet, their eyes focused only on us.

The sallow-faced man began to count and as he did, I hefted the pistol in my hand, getting the feel for its weight and balance.

'One, two, three' . . . came the rhythmic count. My feet moved lightly over the ground, my stride sure and confident.

'Four' . . . the man called and I readied my mind for what I would do. I had decided that with Bontemps, I would turn to my right, first taking a long step to the side so as to be off line from where he expected.

'Five'. . . .

I would then drop to a kneeling position as I brought my pistol to bear. Then, and only then, would I fire. And unlike the others whom André had faced, I would make my shot count.

'Six'. . . .

I stopped, awaiting the command to fire, and when it came I quickly followed my plan, stepping wide to my right and dropping to one knee.

Bontemps now faced me and only a second did he hesitate as he saw me drop to my knee.

I raised my pistol, everything happening in what seemed like slow motion. I saw André shift his gun to his left slightly and down at my position. Our shots sounded as one as the silence of the clearing was rent with the booming thunder of those big bore pistols. I saw André's shirt jump; at the same time I felt a tug at my left shoulder. His bullet had grazed the top of my shoulder causing only a slight flesh wound. My dropping to one knee had caused him to shift his aim before firing, and that slight act had thrown him off just enough.

A warm wetness began to run slowly down my shoulder and even as it did, I rose to my feet.

André's pistol now hung at his side, the smoke from the powder drifting above his head. As I watched, he took a step backwards, stumbling as he did so, then abruptly he sat down in the grass.

His seconds ran to his aid as mine walked up to me, Ring standing by my side.

Bontemps attempted to brush his aides away, but they helped him to his feet anyway. His wound was high on the right side of his chest and his shirtfront was red from the crimson flow.

Ring pulled my shirt back to look at my wound, then said what I already knew about it being only a flesh wound.

While I watched Bontemps' aides work on him, Ring bandaged my wound, having me kneel so he could see better.

When he was finished, I walked over to the cloth on the ground and lay the pistol next to the box. My six-gun and belt had been held for me by one of Ring's men and he proffered it to me now.

Bontemps was hit hard but high, and he would live given proper medical attention. He was on his feet now, although wobbly, and the sallow-faced man stood next to him.

As I watched, André said something to him and the sallow-faced man began to argue. André brushed him off, motioning toward me and my group, and reluctantly he came over to us.

'Monsieur Bontemps,' he said when he arrived, 'wishes to continue. Unless you wish to withdraw, the pistols will be reloaded.'

I turned to Ring and he shrugged his shoulders, saying, 'It is up to you, but decorum allows you to withdraw now with honour. The duel has been fought and both parties must agree for it to continue.'

I looked across the clearing at Bontemps, whose chest and shoulder were heavily bandaged, yet even so blood was beginning to show through their whiteness. A look of pain was on his face, yet so too was one of arrogance and pride.

I returned my gun and gun belt to Ring's man then turned back to the sallow-faced man. 'Reload the pistols,' I said and I stepped back into the center of the clearing.

Once again the pistols were loaded under the watchful eyes of both parties. I had learned one thing and that was that the pistol I had chosen shot slightly high and to my left. Were it not for that, Bontemps would be dead. But I would remember that fault this time.

As we stood face to face again, Ring leaned forward and spoke into my ear.

'You've got him, friend. He can hardly stand now. Take your time and finish him off.'

I nodded impatiently and Ring moved away.

Killing was nothing new to me, yet it was not something that I enjoyed. I would have preferred the duel be over, as I bid no personal ill will towards André Bontemps. He had faced me like a man and had fought honorably. If he wished another chance to redeem himself, then he should have it, and he would get it.

When all parties had resumed their previous positions, the sallow-faced man began to count once more. The count seemed quicker this time, but actually it was the same. My blood was racing, which made things seem faster and clearer.

When he reached six I halted, my pistol held high and ready. When the command came to turn and fire, I whirled around, moving neither to my left or right, nor dropping to my knee as before.

Bontemps was hurried now, knowing his situation, and as I aimed steadily at him, he rushed his shot, the round buzzing by my ear and harmlessly away.

When I realized he had missed, I stopped my finger on the trigger and looked at him. Seeing hesitance, he raised his head proudly and defiantly, as if daring me to shoot.

I remembered then the stories Ring had told, of how others had fired too quickly at André only to miss, and of how he had then practically gloated over them before shooting them down.

I steadied the pistol and re-aimed, the muzzle of the big bore pointing straight at his heart. A twinge of something hit me then, mayhaps mercy, although I found that a discomforting thought. Yet before I fired, I nevertheless raised my aim slightly.

The ugly splat of the .66 caliber chunk of lead was clearly audible as it struck his flesh. This time he dropped to the ground instantly, his body writhing as he fell. Again his aides rushed to his side, and calmly I returned to mine.

Together we stood and watched as André's shirt was torn from him. My bullet, as my last-second action had caused, struck him above the heart and slightly below the collarbone, breaking the clavicle in two.

His pistol lay under the feet of those tending him and his head rolled back and forth as they saw to his wounds.

'It is over, then, is it not?' I asked of Ring.

'That it is,' he answered, 'or at least one would think so. Still,' he went on, 'we must wait.'

'For what?'

'For the announcement from his side that he is dead, or unable to continue. Either will suffice to discontinue the duel.'

Ring's men had gathered around us and we watched as André's wound was patched and bandaged by his aides. Much blood was swabbed away and alcohol was poured liberally over his wound. In spite of all this, and in spite of his previous wound which was bleeding again, André remained conscious. A rolled-up blanket was placed under his head and his aides worked over him feverishly. Surely, I thought, not to prepare him for another round, but to save his life.

He could never stand another turn and if he weren't taken away for the necessary medical treatment, he would die on the spot. Yet I was wrong. The sallow-faced man approached again.

'Monsieur Pickett, Monsieur Bontemps wishes to continue the duel.'

Behind me Ring muttered angrily, his words unworthy of repeating.

'Dot, dammit,' he said, for the first time calling me by my first name. 'Finish the bastard off. Enough is enough. Let's be for getting out of here.'

André had to be helped to his feet as he could barely stand. Each arm was draped over the shoulder of an aide and even as they supported him, he tottered as if about to fall.

When the pistols were presented, though, he stiffened up and as he gripped the handle, I could see his knuckles turn white from the strain.

The count began again and behind me I could hear André's faltering, stumbling step. At six we stopped, and even at twelve paces away, André's ragged, raspy breathing could be clearly heard.

This time, the sallow-faced man did delay, and from the corner of my eye, I could see his face turned towards André.

When the command came, it was as if in desperation. I turned quickly, my pistol held before me.

André was struggling to turn, his feet not working in accord with his desires. When he was almost facing me, his boot heel caught and he tumbled to the ground, landing in a sitting position. Desperately, he struggled to bring his pistol to bear, but despite his efforts to do so, he couldn't.

I jumped when the pistol went off, startled as the slug tore a furrow in the ground not two feet in front of André's body.

Weak and short of blood, he still managed to raise his

eyes to mine. His look was as defiant as ever, and his gaze never wavered.

Turning my pistol to the sky, I fired the round harmlessly away. André's seconds looked surprised, but Ring seemed to have a knowing look on his face.

André Bontemps had been portrayed to me as a heartless man who took pleasure in killing his foe. Although he gave no quarter, he asked for none, either.

A man of his nature would shock the sensibilities of the common man, but within me I felt respect for his courage, if for nothing else. It had not been in me, then, to gun him down as he sat helplessly on the ground. All fighting men, regardless of their personal beliefs, morals or characteristics, respected one common thing, and that common thing was another man's courage.

Although André's men had been surprised at my actions, Ring had not. He knew what I felt and whether he agreed or not, he at least understood. I believe so too did the men with him.

After a short wait, the sallow-faced man came up to us.

'André Bontemps cannot continue. He congratulates you on your victory.'

With that, they loaded André into one of the boats and hastily departed.

I watched silently as they wove among the cypress and soon they were out of sight. When they were gone, we too left the clearing behind.

CHAPTER NINE

The wound to my shoulder was only a bother. It left me stiff and sore, but in no way incapacitated. As I saddled the horse one of Ring's men had brought me, I wondered if André had survived the night with his wounds. What would he do now? What would Antoinette? Daylight was burning and the gold was no closer to its rightful owners than it had been yesterday. And Ring, where was he? When I had risen this morning, he was gone. Was he now trying to delve deeper into this whole matter? Trying to smell out whatever profit he thought might be in this? He was a cagey one, Ring was. And were there a dollar to turn, he'd find a way to do so.

I arrived at the Hilliard Plantation nigh on to lunch and it was evil stares that greeted me. The butler who had greeted Ring and me before came down the steps with a stare cold enough to freeze nails.

'What do you seek here, Monsieur?' he asked, his voice as hostile as Comanches on a blood trail.

'I wish to speak with Miss Thibodeaux. It is time for this matter to come to an end.'

Before he could reply, a voice spoke from behind me. I turned on the saddle and looked straight into the twin eyes of an ugly-looking shotgun. This man I had not seen before, and if ever a man had murder in his eyes, this man did.

'You are not welcome here,' he said. 'Leave the premises now, or be buried where you stand.'

A stumbling step at the head of the stairs caused us all to turn in that direction. It was André Bontemps, tottering precariously on a cane, his chest bandaged from neck to navel.

'That's enough, Pierre,' he spoke gently. The man Pierre turned and stomped away, the shotgun held at his side.

I turned back to André as he spoke. 'Antoinette is not here. She was gone when I returned yesterday.' His voice had a hint of sadness in it and strangely I found myself believing him. It was something just as this that I had feared. While I had been out deciding 'matters of honor', Antoinette had fled with the gold. And what of Ring's men? They were supposed to watch for just such as this.

'It seems you may have been right, Monsieur Pickett. About your property, I mean. One of the livery informed me that Antoinette left hurriedly, taking one of my best horses and another carrying her valise and a pair of saddle-bags.'

He left it hanging there, and I knew he purposely left off 'heavy saddle-bags'.

The butler had left now and only André and I occupied the tarmac in front of his sprawling plantation house.

Somewhat reflectively, he said, 'Ah, women. They have turned the heads of many men better than I. A pretty face, a petulant smile, a voice like silk. It is enough, my friend, to make men kill, is it not?'

Having been duped myself, I knew the feeling and voiced as much.

'Well, let bygones be bygones,' André said, calling over his shoulder for the man, Pierre. When he arrived, André ordered. 'Bring up Star from the stables. Put Monsieur Pickett's rig on him and turn this crow bait of Ring's in the pasture.'

Pierre cast a stunned look at André, his face incredulous

with disbelief.

'Star,' André went on, speaking to me, 'is the fastest horse in all of the parishes. If Antoinette can be caught, Star will catch her. Besides,' he went on, smiling knowingly, 'the horse she took is Star's colt. Get within a mile of her and Star will lead you home.' He turned to leave, but stopped as I spoke.

'*Merci*, André,' and I meant it, for even as I spoke, I could see the mare being led up by Pierre. The horse Ring had provided was no match for this long-legged high-stepping mare.

André waved casually over his shoulder. 'Good luck,' he said softly as he hobbled inside.

Quickly, I unsaddled and threw my gear on the mare. She tossed her head and pranced about impatiently, taking the bit like a hound on a spoor. This was a travelling horse and although most western men wouldn't ride a mare, this one was well worth the exception.

I lit a shuck out of there and glad I was to go. I didn't like the look of Pierre and a couple of loads in the back from that shotgun had no place in my plans.

Where to go now and what to do? In the plains or hills I was at home and would have put my nose to the trail and tracked her down. But I was no city man and a girl like Antoinette would be hard to figure. Would she hide out in New Orleans proper? Or would she flee altogether? Would she head for the French Quarter hoping to be swallowed up by its secret folds? I thought not, as that girl wanted away from André and from those who knew her. She wanted to spend that gold, not hatch it. And could she not do it in New Orleans, she would find some other suitable place. I must move fast, and I knew it, else I would lose her to some big city. San Francisco, Denver, St Louis, all would beckon to her and the gold would ride heavy on her mind.

I prowled the streets of New Orleans the rest of the day, checking the train stations, the docks, liveries that rented rigs – all to no avail. Antoinette had taken two horses, I had assumed only to reach town, but mayhap I was wrong. Did she plan to travel cross-country? I would have said no, but I could find no one who had seen a girl fitting her description. Did she have help, co-conspirators, what? As dusk settled on the city, I began to give up hope. I had lost her. I knew not where to turn. It was in this moment of despair that I glimpsed a familiar face. It was Ring. Ring of the knives, Ring of the rings in his ears, Ring of the 'I know something you don't' smile on his face. He stepped off the sidewalk and sauntered up to me, the rings in his ears flashing in the waning light.

'*Mon ami* Pickett, I have looked high and low for you. Where have you been?'

At my stare and silence to his question he chuckled, knowing full well where I had been.

'I see you have a mount, and quite a mount at that. Did you steal the mare?' he asked, needling me.

'That is more in your line of work, Ring,' I answered tiredly. 'She was a gift to me from your friend Bontemps.'

He chuckled again and asked, 'Do you look for the lady with two horses, and the saddle-bags that make her stumble from their weight?'

He had my attention then and well he knew it. His smile broadened and it did my mood no good to see him so proud of himself.

'Have you seen her?'

He nodded, for all in the world looking like a cat with its paws full of mice.

'She is leaving even as we speak. Nothing escapes Ring. Do you forget what I tell you? Come, come,' he beckoned. 'Before she leaves us far behind.'

So it was 'us' now, I wondered to myself. But it was Ring who held the cards and I followed him as he wove his way among the darkened streets that interlaced this fabled city.

A full moon shone on us as we followed the trail Antoinette had left. Surprisingly to me, she had quickly fled the protective folds of New Orleans, making her way into the rough country surrounded by the murky bayous. Her trail was not aimless and she wandered not at all, leaving both Ring and I with the opinion that she had a specific destination in mind. Her trail, because of this, was easy to follow. Although Ring was a man of the swamps and bayous, it was I who led, and I bandied not about. Did Ring get left behind then his misfortune was his own.

When New Orleans was twenty miles behind us, I pulled up and stepped down for a breather. Ring followed suit and although he tried not to show it, I could tell the rapidity of our travel had taken some starch out of him. Bayou born and bred he may be, but when it came to making tracks and making them abundantly, horseback was obviously not his trump card. He sat down on an up-thrusting stump as I built a fire, and gingerly did he sit. At my chuckle, he cast me an angry look, but I ignored him and built a fire.

It was beautiful here in the swamps, but my eyes had no time for beauty now. We drank our coffee quickly, allowing the horses a chance to blow and drink themselves, then forked our saddles and lit out. Another two hours brought us clear of the bayous and on to dry, elevated land. At the same time, my eyes caught a flicker of light, and signaling to Ring I pulled up and peered across a slight clearing. A fire burned brazenly and sitting around it were three men – and Antoinette Thibodeaux. They were about fifty yards across the clearing and we fifty yards from the clearing itself. From one hundred yards away, I easily recognized the three men.

They were Caxton Banks, his brother Everson, and the man who had been with them in Abilene. How they had gotten here I couldn't say, and how Antoinette had joined with them was just as big a mystery. Perhaps they had been in cahoots from the start. Someone had put Antoinette on to us in the first place. Had it been Caxton? Had he wired ahead to her, alerting her of my coming and what to do? Was this the place they were to meet all along if Antoinette was successful in her mission? Evidently so, for there they sat, as big as day.

Tying our horses back a hundred yards from the clearing, Ring and I crept around to within twenty yards of the fire. The Banks brothers were laughing and drinking, toasting their good fortune. Antoinette was just as revelling, as was the third man whose name I still did not know. They were having a grand old time and at their feet, plainly visible by the blazing light of the fire, lay the valise that Antoinette had used to steal the gold, its contents spilled out and around them. Ring noticed this as well as I, and the little bags would surely confirm his growing suspicions.

Silently, we watched the quartet celebrate. Caxton was nigh on a drunk and his voice was loud and clearly audible.

'San Francisco, my friends. A grand time we'll have there. The city will be yours, Antoinette, and with a stake like this, there will be no stopping us.'

They all laughed and drank another round; that is with the exception of Antoinette, who drank not at all.

Everson chimed in, 'That Pickett was a canny one and near gave us the slip. But, alas, who has the gold now?'

Raucous laughter followed again.

'When Frank gets here, he'll be fit to be tied,' Caxton said.

'Thought we couldn't do it, but who has the last laugh now?'

Who was Frank, I wondered, as that name I had not heard before.

Ring, his eyes as big as eggs on a plate, stared unblinkingly at the gold and the men who surrounded it. Were I able to dispossess it from Caxton and his group, I would then have to deal with Ring. This I knew, as Ring was a persistent man. He was biding. Biding his time till the right opportunity availed itself. Then he would strike, I knew, but only then. For now, he was content to play along with me, as two men could recover the gold far more easily than one. In so doing, the odds would be whittled more to his liking.

My idea, right then and there, was to charge the camp, guns blazing, and retake the gold on the spot. I had had enough of this dilly-dallying across Louisiana and like the old man said, time was a-wasting.

I motioned to Ring and my intent must have shown in my eyes, for he shook his head and put a finger to his lips. I started to protest. Yet before I could, the sound of a horse tramping through the land behind the clearing silenced me. A moment later, the horse and rider broke the clearing, those around the fire standing up in greeting as Caxton uttered one word: 'Frank!'

This man, too, I knew, but awhile it took me to place him. He wore buckskins with worn riding boots on his feet, a floppy hat sat on his head and in his hand, waving lazily by his leg, was a rifle. He sat his horse like a man accustomed to many miles in the saddle, and the way he carried his rifle bespoke a man familiar in its ways.

Gone were the glasses he had worn before and the portly look he had once had suddenly seemed quite different. More so a look of a man who had heavy, but heavy with muscles in the arms, chest and stomach. A man who had power, not only physically, but mentally as well. This man whom Caxton had called Frank was the banker from

Abilene. The man I knew only as Gattis. He himself, who had packed the gold for me and had me sign the receipt. So, way back then my suspicions had been correct. The banker had informed Caxton of the gold. Well, no wonder folks were distrustful of bankers.

'Light and set, Frank,' Caxton said, a look of pride on his face.

Frank stepped down, the rifle still at his side, and using the barrel he pointed at the saddle-bag with its contents in plain sight.

'Is that the gold?' he asked.

'Sure 'nough,' Caxton answered. 'Just like we promised. It's all there, too, Frank. Every last ounce.'

Frank moved over to the saddle-bags and using the rifle, turned over a few of the bags.

Slowly, he turned back to Caxton, 'Good job, boys. I knew you could do it. You've made me proud.'

'Thanks, Uncle Frank,' Everson said, 'only one thing left to be done.'

Frank looked at Everson coldly, an expression of raw hate on his face.

'Quite right,' he answered, nodding in agreement. 'Now we must kill Dot Pickett and bury him deep. But first we will have our fun with him, right, boys?'

All the men nodded in agreement with Frank, hard looks on every face.

So the man named Gattis was actually Frank, and Frank was an uncle to Caxton and Everson. This, then, must be Franklin J. Banks. I had heard his name before, in Dodge City, shortly after my battle with the three Banks boys at Doan's. Franklin J. Banks was their father. The father of the men I had killed, and all the while in Abilene he had counted out the gold to me knowing that across from him stood the man who had killed his sons, all three of them.

The thought fair made my skin crawl and a shiver ran over me, one so strong it caused Ring to look at me with wonder.

After Frank's arrival, the revelry ended. The men gathered around the fire, their heads together in some evil plot, presumably against me. Surely they believed me to still be in New Orleans and if my guess were right, Frank Banks was more interested in revenge than the gold. Caxton and Everson would evidently follow Frank's lead, but whether revenge was a primary motivation on their part, I could not say.

Gold would speak loud to them and I doubted if they would continue in any prolonged plot to avenge the deaths of their cousins. Like as not, as they had intimated earlier, they would as soon be off to San Francisco and the fine times they envisioned there.

As I ran these thoughts through my mind, Antoinette rose and excused herself from the men who still huddled around the fire. Catching Ring's attention, I signalled for him to keep watch as I quickly made my way in the direction where Antoinette had disappeared in the surrounding woods. Bullfrogs croaked their timbric calls over the night, and cicadas whirred wistfully from the trees that rose eerily from the moss-laden earth. Soon I closed on Antoinette, who made no effort to disguise her movements. When I had positioned myself between her and the safety of those gathered back in the clearing, I stepped from behind a gnarled cypress tree and stood full in the light of the moon. Even so, it was a while before she spotted me and when she did, her hand flew to her face, her suddenly trembling fingers covering her open mouth.

'So we meet again, Miss Thibodeaux. You seem a bit surprised.'

She recovered her composure quickly, a feigned smile

91

coming to her face.

'Yes, it is a surprise. We thought you were still in New Orleans.' Nervously, she looked around, her eyes seeking those at the fire. 'How did you find me?' she asked.

'Never mind that. I've come for the gold. The gold you stole from me and from the people it rightly belongs to.'

Her eyes sought the ground and she shuffled her feet nervously.

'It has been a long trail,' I continued, 'but now the journey is nearing its end. Too many people have been hurt already and enough blood has been shed. Return the gold, Antoinette, and I'll guarantee you safe passage out of here.'

'They would never accept that,' she said, nodding towards the clearing. 'Frank wants you dead and the rest want the gold. I have no say in any of this.'

She looked at me, and once again her beauty struck me. I could not understand how one of her ilk could become involved with the likes of the Banks boys, nor, for that matter, André Bontemps. I voiced as much, and she replied.

'Frank and my father rode together in the war. My father was killed at Bull Run and when the war was over, Frank came to tell my mother and I. During the war, Frank's wife passed of consumption and eventually he married my mother, bringing his three sons with him.'

She paused a moment, her eyes far away in reflection.

'Frank was far from being an ideal stepfather and after my own mother passed away, things quickly became unbearable. I was treated as if I was a nobody and made to wait hand and foot on the lot of them. Finally,' she said, taking a deep breath before continuing, 'I ran away and came to New Orleans. It was there that I met André. And being penniless and without work, he took me in. From day one he tried to love me, and his actions and intentions were always honorable. I had no place else to go, but even so, I would not accept André's proposals. My refusals did not deter him, however, yet he always remained a gentleman.

'Being unwed, though, and living under the same roof, rumors began to flow. My reputation, as it were, became tainted and most viewed me as André's mistress. This was not so, but people will talk.

'André said he was in love with me, but I was not with him. I wanted to leave but had nowhere to go. By this time, Frank and his sons had left our home in Virginia and became involved in cattle rustling and robbing ranchers of their herd money. One day in New Orleans, I ran into Caxton. I hadn't seen him in years, so we had coffee and talked. This was over a year ago, and then, just a few weeks back, he wired me about you and advised that I try to intercept you should you come this way. He described you and the two men with you and although he admitted it was a long shot, I took it as the opportunity I needed to get away from New Orleans and André Bontemps. Luck have it, the very day I arrived at Alexandria, I saw you and recognized you. Well,' she laughed nervously, shrugging her shoulders, 'you know the rest.'

'And here we stand,' I concluded. She only nodded, her hand dabbing at a wet eye. She reached into her tiny handbag – for a handkerchief, I assumed – and at point blank range, she shot me.

CHAPTER TEN

Before the sound of the shot died on the sullen night, and even before I half fell–half dived for the cover of the gnarled cypress, pandemonium broke out from the clearing. Shots rent the night with their sharp staccato bursts and people could be heard cursing and running for cover.

Antoinette was gone. She had vanished into the thick growth of trees as quietly as a ghost.

Quickly, I rolled over, drawing my pistol as I did. I was shot, all right, high in the left shoulder; a glancing blow that cut an ugly gash in my flesh sending a torrent of blood cascading down my shirt and over my chest.

A crashing, stumbling step came towards me. It was the man who had been with Caxton and Everson in Abilene. His gun was drawn and he peered intently over his shoulder as he came. Too late he saw me, and as he tried to bring his gun to bear, I fired. His hands flew high, his pistol cartwheeling off into the air as he pitched headlong to the ground. He was dead, and I left him there.

Shots still came from the clearing and a horse ran past me, the stirrups bouncing wildly as the sorrel fled the gunfire that had frightened him.

And then, as quickly as that, the night was once again silent; not a peep nor a sound from any direction.

I began to make my way around to where I had last seen Ring. As I neared the clearing, I could see one body sprawled on its side next to the fire. It was Everson Banks, and he was dead.

My horse was still there, tethered securely to a live oak as thick as my waist.

Where was Ring? Now in pursuit of Frank and Caxton? Or more aptly, in pursuit of the gold?

I could hear nothing in the night about me; everyone had vanished.

Then I heard the cry of an owl. Strange, I thought, that after all the shots and raucous noise of a moment ago an owl would pierce the silence with its lonely hoot. Were it a wise owl, as I had heard owls to be, it would have fled at the first shot.

On a hunch, I went to the sound. Not long after, my intuition paid off, for there sat Ring, a pistol in each hand, the rings in his ear twinkling under the light of the moon.

I sat my horse next to his and, like he, listened intently for any sound. Quietly, we walked our horses in the direction Ring had seen Frank and Caxton disappear.

After shooting me, Antoinette had circled around and caught up her horse just in time to join Frank and Caxton as they fled the clearing. They had waited on her, but as Ring had said, were they any slower she would have rode right up their shirt tails.

On mutual agreement Ring and I split up, he taking an arc from the west, and I from the east. In this pincer movement we hoped to intercept or cut off those who fled before us.

It was touch and go traveling through here, as the lowland was interspersed with sloughs, bayous, cypress thickets and bogs that would sink a horse to his brisket. Neither sight nor sound, hide nor hair did I see of the Bankses, and after an hour of this pattern, I drew up. The night was still silent and the moon was beginning to wane.

As agreed upon by Ring and me, I did my best to imitate an owl, such things not being among my better talents. After the third try, an answer came from far to my left. Ten minutes later, Ring and I were back together.

'They are about a mile from us, holed up in a shack next to a slough. A bayou runs in a half-circle around it and there's only one way in – straight down the muzzle of their guns.'

'Let's go, then,' I said, motioning for Ring to lead the way. 'Let's get this over with once and for all.'

Ring only sat his horse and I pulled up in exasperation.

'There's seven guns there, Dot, not counting the girl. A lean-to just behind the shack holds five horses – eight now, counting theirs. I got close enough to see inside and there's five pretty salty-looking customers inside. A couple I recognized – Sawyer Bates and Hondo Cain.'

I had never heard of Sawyer Bates, but if Ring had, he must be someone to reckon with. Hondo Cain was another story. I had heard of him in Dodge, Abilene and Ellsworth. Hondo Cain, the Kansas badman. The pistoleer of the prairies. He was called 'Pistol' for his dexterity with such, but he was almost as well-known for his feats with his fists. He had taken Goff Ford's pistol from him in Ellsworth and beat him to a frazzle. A week or so later Ford came at him again, only this time he stayed far enough away that pistols were the only choice. He shot Goff Ford right between the eyes.

'From the looks of it,' Ring went on, 'their five gun hands have been holed up back there for a couple of days, just waiting. Seems like someone did a bit of planning here. They must want you pretty bad and they must also feel it's going to take more than a few guns to get you.'

Ring was smiling at me, seemingly enjoying the predicament we were now in. The more the odds rose, the more he smiled. The more danger we were in, the more he smiled. The day they lay him in his grave, Ring would be smiling. To be truthful, it was kinda aggravating, all this damn smiling.

As I contemplated this, a voice sounded behind us. He spoke in French and I understood not a word, but the cocking of his rifle was a sound universally understood.

Another rifle sounded in front of us; this sound that of a shell being levered into a chamber.

'Hold tight, *mon ami*,' Ring said. 'I think they have us fairly trapped!'

I should reckon so, I thought, sitting here in the moonlight like two tenderfeet from the big city.

Ring said something in French and this time the voice spoke in English.

'Just sit tight there, boys. There's been enough gunshots disturbing my sleep tonight as is. The gun in front of you is Toby and Toby don't miss what Toby shoots at.'

The man's voice was heavily accented and quite old, it seemed, but his rifle was young and full of vinegar. We sat as told and the old man closed with us, still keeping to our backside.

'Toby,' he called. 'Relieve these gents of their hardware so we can get a good look at them.'

A small form came forward at his command and quickly took Ring's pistols from him. I watched out of the corner of my eye as the boy came toward me. A hat too big sat on his head and a baggy shirt hung halfway to his knees, covering the better part of his raggedy, holey britches. The boy was barefoot and the paleness of his feet stood out starkly in the light of the moon. I could not see his face, as he kept his head down. And as he reached up to take my pistol, my hand shot out and covered his, squeezing tight and crushing his

97

slender fingers against the butt. A muffled sound of pain came from his mouth and the old man spoke behind me.

'Careful there, mister. This rifle will put a hole through you big enough to jump a horse through.'

Nonetheless, I refused to relinquish my hold and the boy squirmed under my grip.

'Old timer, you shoot me in the back if you must, but I'll not give up my gun. There's too many in these swamps that'd kill me given half a chance. If I die, I'll die with my gun on me.'

He chuckled, his voice cackling like an old hen's.

'They be that, don't they, boy? Been keeping my eye on them for a couple of days. Caught most of your shindig back to the clearing, too. That girl,' he went on, chuckling even louder, 'she sure 'nough shot you. Slick as a whistle, she were. Thought you was going to break your neck diving behinst that tree after she plugged you.' He cackled again and I wondered where in tarnation he had been when all this was going on. I sure never saw him and that in itself said something for his ability to move about in these bottom-lands.

'Come away from there, Toby. Let the man keep his gun. We wouldn't want to be the cause of his being murdered, now would we?'

The boy didn't answer and a moment later I let go of his hand. He backed up, stumbling, rubbing his aching fingers as he went, almost dropping his rifle as he tried to hold it.

'My friend's guns, too,' I said. 'He's just as big a target as I.'

At some apparent signal from the old man, whom I still couldn't see, the boy returned Ring's guns to him, ignoring his flashing smile and courteous '*merci*!'

The old man walked past us, his rifle hanging at his side. He motioned for us to follow him, saying over his shoulder,

'There's coffee on if you want some.' I looked at Ring, who only shrugged. The boy fell in behind the old man, and Ring and I followed suit.

It was a winding, twisting route we followed, the old man leading us through a maze of trails and footpaths. But soon we came to a hut nestled neatly between two huge cypress trees. Coon skins, 'possum skins and snake skins hung from racks and boards, these drying forms almost covering the porch that ran the length of the hut, which we faced. Tarpaper covered the windows and Spanish moss hung from the limbs of the huge cypresses clear to the top of the hut. A thick, tangled growth of trees and vines abutted the hind-most of the hut, leaving it only visible from where we now gazed, and did we move ten feet in any direction, the hut would be entirely invisible.

Arbuckle coffee cans, flattened by a hammer into a patch of sorts, were nailed strategically to the hut, their dented red shapes covering holes in the planks that were the walls of this structure. Some were on the porch, too, the red worn off of the tin planks from the constant scuffing of feet.

Traps, chains, washtubs and wooden cages hung from the outer walls of the hut and placed around these were tools, their shapes hanging from broken, rusty nails. This hut was old – very old; but for all its outward look of shabbiness, it was snug and well-hidden. A better place to hide a man would go far to find.

The coffee was hot and strong, and the old man full of conversation. He had lived in this shack for nigh on to sixty years, earning a living by trapping while living off the land as best he could. Here in the bayous of the bottomland, that would be a bountiful existence, as fresh seafood and fresh water fish were abundant. Also plentiful were crawdads, turtles and all sorts of waterfowl. Yet, even so, this was a secluded, lonely life, at least for the youngster. As I shared stories with the two of them of cattle drives, gunmen, outlaws and cow towns, the boy's eyes stared at me in big-eyed wonder. When I talked of New Orleans and all the sights and sounds there, the boy could hardly contain himself as he sat on a stool back in the dark corner. From what the old man said, this was his grandchild, left for him to raise when he was only two. Seems the two of them had never been out of the bayous, least not in the boy's lifetime, and I could understand the boy's longing for tales of the 'other' world.

After the pleasantries were over and after three cups of coffee were under my belt, I began to pump the old man for what he knew and had seen of the men now with the Bankses and Antoinette. He was a willing talker, seemingly in love with the sound of his own voice, and he began his rendition happily.

They had arrived two days back, along with Frank. They moved in to the old shack, long ago abandoned, and had waited there while Everson and Caxton set up camp at the clearing. Seems this clearing had been used before and was known as a meeting place for transactions in illegal business. The old man, being sly and suspicious at the same time, kept an eye on the goings-on and happened to be out and about when the shooting broke out. This neck of the woods was his stomping grounds and he seemed some put out at the thought of city folks tromping about and shooting up the place.

'That shack where them boys be holed up,' he said, his old, gnarled hands twisting in his lap, his eyes sparkling with so much attention, 'is set just right for defences. You two would have a hard time flushing them boys out of there less'n they wanted to be flushed. Won't do you much good to be off chasin' after them tonight.

'Come mornin' they'll be moving out anyhows. There's eight of them, counting that girl, and there's only two of you. With them odds, they'll not ride scared.'

While he talked, the boy cleaned the gash in my shoulder from Antoinette's gun. The wound was nasty, but only a flesh wound, and once cleaned and bandaged, it would be all right.

There was something disconcerting about this boy, for he never spoke and constantly kept his eyes lowered, never looking you right in the face. He knew his business at cleaning wounds, though, and I passed off his quirks as shyness around strangers.

The old man prattled on about this and that, while Ring lay sleeping on one of the bunks. My head was nodding and my eyes were doing their best to put an end to the day. Under the gentle ministrations of the boy, it was all I could do to stay awake.

Forcing myself out of my drowsiness, I stood and stretched the stiffness from my bones. The old man stopped in mid-sentence, looking at me questioningly.

'I better see to the horses,' I said. 'It's been a long day for them, too.'

He nodded and called for Toby to give me a hand.

I unsaddled Star as well as Ring's horses, giving the saddles to Toby, who propped them on the porch.

His hands were slender and delicate and his bare feet were small, almost dainty, with tiny pink toes. Having never got a clear look at his face I couldn't estimate his age, but he was the shyest, quietest boy I had ever known. Feeling somewhat sorry for the boy, I slapped him on the shoulder and roughed his hat affectionately. My hand caused the boy's floppy old hat to fall from his head and he turned to face me quickly, a look of fear in his eyes. His hair, free from the restraints of the hat, fell about his shoulders in long, golden curls. He must have seen the surprise and shock on my face, for he turned hastily and fled into the hut. My surprise and shock were well reasoned, for Toby was a girl and a right pretty one at that.

It took me a moment to gather my wits. When I entered the hut, Ring was snoring away on a cot, while Toby and the old man huddled in a corner. At my entrance, they both peered my way and then the girl rose and came forward. Gone was the timidity of before, as now that her secret was exposed she walked proudly, the floppy hat gone from her head and her face full to view. She was, in fact, quite pretty. Long golden curls fell daintily about her shoulders and her eyes were blue with a sparkle that made itself evident even in the hut lighted only by the flickering light of a beat-up coal oil lamp.

'My name is Tobiatha,' she said, holding her long, slender fingers out to me.

I took her hand gently, mindful of the fingers I had crushed earlier.

'My grandfather is Henry Carboneau. I am sorry for the masquerade, but we live alone out here and most of the men who pass by are rough and wild. The disguise was my grandpa's idea. A means by which to avoid trouble before it starts.'

'I understand, miss,' I said, smiling at her pretty face. 'It's probably a good idea, as alone and away from the law, some men are apt to do most anything.'

'I'm glad you understand, as it is against my nature to be deceitful, but, well,' she said, shrugging her shoulders, 'this is a rough country and one must adapt to survive.'

Henry Carboneau, apparently satisfied at the direction of our conversation, lay down on another bunk against the far wall, his hat pulled over his eyes.

We talked a good while, Toby and I, as she was full of interest for the things outside of her tiny world. I did my best to tell her of New Orleans and the sights and sounds of the city, and later I found myself telling her about my childhood; the death of my parents and the subsequent moving from place to place I had then endured. I talked of my first cattle drive, of long hours of practice with a pistol, and of friendships later forged through gun battles and long hours on the trail.

Naturally I explained my current problems to her fully, and when I mentioned the part about Antoinette's betrayal and theft of the gold, her eyes filled with a sullen anger. When I later mentioned how smitten I had been by Antoinette's striking beauty, the sullen anger in Tobiatha's eyes became liquid in its intensity, her increased agitation as plain to see as the moon in the sky.

As Ring snored loudly in the corner, Toby told me her own story. She barely remembered her mother, and her father not at all. Her mother's name had been Marie, and they had lived on the outskirts of New Orleans. Her father was a no-account gambler named Francois Malveau. He was killed in a gambling hall when Toby was only a year old, and her mother had then joined her father, Toby's grandfather, Henry Carboneau, in the edges of the swamp. Marie Malveau had taken ill with a fever of some sort and slowly but surely dwindled away, first losing her energy and drive, then her colour and senses, and finally, when Toby was barely two years old, her mother had at last passed away, and Henry Carboneau had taken charge of the toddling youngster.

Toby quickly became a tomboy, ranging far and wide in her explorations of the bayous and swamplands that practically surrounded their hut and small clearing. She became self-sufficient and very independent in her tiny world, and Henry Carboneau had been content to give her her head. She was safe enough, as they were well off the beaten path, and the only people who penetrated their solitary world were

Cajun trappers and traders who passed through from time to time, providing sustenance to their diet by trading salt, flour, coffee and sugar to old man Carboneau for furs, fish, 'gator skins and whatever else he happened to catch or find.

Toby had only met or seen in her entire life ten men at most until our arrival, an arrival that coincided with that of the Banks crowd and Antoinette. Her world, so to speak, had been doubled in one fell swoop – at least as far as humans were concerned.

I found her existence hard to conceive. Toby was a pretty girl. Not strikingly beautiful like Antoinette, but pretty in a strong way. How she had coped with the solitude and loneliness that she must have borne was beyond me. The emptiness it had created was all too apparent, as Toby hung on every word I said and everything I did. Her questions were boundless and soon the sheer volume of them wore me to utter exhaustion.

Her innocence was quite charming, though, and stirred a protective feeling in me that I had never felt before. When Toby told me her age, I was surprised. She was seventeen. Born the same year and month as I, although she was unsure of the exact date. I would have guessed her as younger, no more than fifteen, but what could I tell of a girl in beat-up pants and a ragged shirt? She didn't even wear shoes, but even so there was a sureness and beauty about her that I couldn't describe.

Small though she was, and naïve and innocent to boot, something about Toby assured me in some way that she could fend for herself. If only one of us was left alive after all was said and done here, something told me it would be her. I couldn't put a finger on it, but Toby was like a wild creature, alert to every sound and movement around her, in tune with everything that happened in her world and near it. That world, of course, now included me.

CHAPTER ELEVEN

The next morning found us up early, but even so, both Toby and her grandfather were already drinking coffee and sitting by a handful of fire. Toby was slicing salt pork into a pot of rice, and fresh biscuits sat steaming on a makeshift table. My stomach growled hungrily and I hurried to join our two new friends at the table, Ring only a moment behind me. He grinned when he saw Toby, realizing that his suspicions about her had been correct all along.

After we had eaten, I laid out my plans for the day. I wanted to scout the cabin where Ring had trailed Frank and Caxton banks along with Antoinette. Carboneau told us that the cabin was known as 'Smuggler's Cabin', as years ago smugglers and pirates had used it as a hiding place while their captains and officers were about in New Orleans. It had been many years, he said, since anyone had used it, other than himself. And he had been surprised two days ago to find it occupied by five 'bad looking' men.

When Ring had first spied the cabin and its occupants, he had recognized two: Sawyer Bates, from Natchez-Under-The-Hill, and Hondo Cain, the Kansas Badman. The other three were unknown to us, but simply to ride with the Bankses marked them as dangerous men. If in fact the cabin was as defendable as Carboneau had assured us, there was little that Ring and I could do to flush them out. But they were seven men and one young woman. They were also in possession of the gold. They had no reason to seek asylum in an old smuggler's cabin on the edges of a swamp. They had places to go and things to do, and two men they desperately wanted to kill. I was at the top of the list, and the father of the three men I had killed was here in these very woods and swamps seeking a father's vengeance. Ring would be next, at least in priority, as he had killed Caxton's brother Everson just last night. If I judged Caxton right, the gold and San Francisco would call louder to him than vengeance for his brother. But Frank would keep them on track, and until Ring and I were dead, no one would be leaving this wild tangle of wetland – gold or no gold.

I wanted to see the cabin myself, and try to discover the plans of the Bankses. I felt they would be out in search of us first thing, perhaps even now, and although I felt relatively safe here, I didn't want to bring the hounds to the fox, so to speak, as at this moment, Henry Carboneau and his presence was unknown to the Bankses. I doubted if anyone in their group could track us here, as gunmen weren't generally known as trackers. But three of the five gunmen with the Bankses were unknown to us, and to assume too much could cost us our lives, as well as those of Henry Carboneau and Toby.

With this in mind, we saddled up and left our two friends behind. Toby had wanted to go with us, claiming she could scout ahead of us and stay out of sight. But Carboneau would have none of it, although he himself did follow us up the trail and away from his cabin, obliterating all sign of our passage both coming and going.

A small cluster of whitetail deer grazed peacefully in a small clearing as we passed silently by. Ring rode quietly as did I, and he led the way cautiously through the low-lying

106

brush and undergrowth, picking his way through the thickets of trees and tangles of vines that hindered our progress over a barely discernible trail that seemingly wove haphazardly up and over a slight rise.

Tiny flowers grew among the mesh of vines, brush and grass, their colours bright and pleasant, but their names a mystery to me. The birds that darted here and there were the same; unknown and different to me, yet beautiful and pleasing to see. I found myself wondering at the differences in the land here and that of my home in Washington, Texas, and once again found myself struck by a yearning to experience and explore more of this country that I lived in.

A whisper from Ring woke me from my reverie and I pulled up next to him, both of us listening and peering intently ahead. After a moment he motioned me off to his right, and we spread out slightly, about twenty yards apart.

As we crested the slight rise warily, a scant three-quarters of a mile from Carboneau's cabin, a rider could be seen in the distance. His eyes were on the ground, searching for something or following someone. Once again I pulled up next to Ring and we hid behind a collection of close-growing trees, undetectable to the rider slightly below us. He came on and we watched silently.

When he was about a half mile away, Ring leaned toward me and said, 'He's following my trail from yesterday. I passed through that low spot before cutting back up here to catch the trail.'

It was obvious from the direction he was taking that he would soon cross our newest trail, and by doing so would locate and verify our position.

We could pass by him by moving off to our left and following a line of trees that would conceal us from his sight, but when he found our new trail, he would turn and follow us, putting him behind us and effectively pinching us between himself and the cabin ahead of us.

We could stop and kill him, but the shots would alert those ahead of us and spoil any chance of surprise and undo any opportunity to scout the cabin and those set against us.

We moved off and left to pass on. By the time he found our trail and turned about, he would be a good half hour behind us.

I still hadn't formulated a plan. Seven men against two were heavy odds, and there was also Antoinette to consider. She had already proven herself capable of killing, as the wound and bandage on my neck confirmed. If she bore arms against me again, what would I do? What could I do? Could I kill a woman? Even in the defence of my own life, or that of Ring's, could I shoot a woman? I would never have thought that I'd find myself debating such an issue, but it was a very real possibility. Antoinette had taken cards in this game, and I had no doubt she would see it through until the very end.

Suddenly three more riders appeared, taking us both by surprise, and we drew up in tandem, our horses tossing their heads at the sharp bite of the bits. We moved not a stitch, as these riders were almost on top of us and I prayed silently that our horses would not give us away. They stood fast, seeming to sense our trepidation, and as soon as the riders had appeared, they were gone, following approximately the path taken by the first rider we had come by.

When they were safely gone, we moved on once again. Ring said the cabin was close, just through the next patch of trees. We sought a place to hide our horses, and thus unencumbered moved ahead on foot. Ring was like a ghost in his movements, his every step silent and attentive, while the going was more difficult for me. I was a plainsman, not a woodsman, but nevertheless I did my best to follow Ring's example and not give away our presence by knocking over a tree.

Four men were gone from the cabin now; the first rider who had been following Ring's trail of the night before and the three riders who had just recently passed us by. None of these had been Sawyer Bates or Hondo Cain, the two most dangerous of the gunmen retained by Frank and Caxton Banks. The four of them must now be together along with Antoinette. If they were together in the cabin, this could possibly be the best chance we'd ever have to dispossess them of the gold. Their force was effectively cut in half, and if we moved swiftly, perhaps we could end this here and now.

A lazy trail of gray smoke split a soft blue sky as Ring and I at last drew in sight of the cabin. It was well hidden amongst the trees, built of natural materials, which only aided in obscuring its presence from the casual eye. A small window in the back faced us and some type of cloth material blocked its tiny opening.

As we inched closer, a woman's laughter broke the silence, then a man's muffled, stern voice replied.

I moved up to the wall of the cabin, the window just beside my head, and signalled for Ring to stay where he was. Although I could hear voices inside, I couldn't quite make them out but that they were planning something was obvious. Antoinette was attempting to convince someone, probably Frank, to pack up the gold and leave. But from the snatches of conversation I did hear, he was adamant that they must 'clean things up' before anyone went anywhere.

Then a voice spoke almost in my ear, and I heard every word clearly. 'Dot's a dead man, Antoinette. I swear that by all that's holy, him and his damn Cajun friend! Corbin will find their trail and we'll flush them from their hiding place. Once we've shovelled the dirt in their faces, we'll all get the hell out of here. But until then, we'll have no more talk of the gold. Do I make myself clear?'

From the corner of my eye I saw the curtain move and the

side of a face appeared in the frame. I froze instantly as it was Frank Banks. And if he turned in my direction even slightly, he would see me. He was peering into the trees and I prayed that Ring was out of sight. Frank spoke then, and the closeness of his voice made my skin crawl.

'This place gives me the willies! The sooner we're shut of it, the better! This land isn't fit for anything but a bunch of damn swamp rats!'

The curtain moved again and the face disappeared. I breathed a sigh of relief and eased my hand from the butt of my pistol.

Only a while longer I listened at the window, but it was enough to place all four men and Antoinette inside. I rejoined Ring and told him my idea.

'If you can get around to their horses and run them off, I may have a chance to get inside. If not, at least we can put them afoot until the others return.'

Neither of us had seen the horses, but the back of a dilapidated lean-to could be seen just on the other side of the cabin. If Ring could Injun around and get inside, he could turn the horses loose and run them off. They probably wouldn't go far, but any distance would buy us time.

'If their saddles are in the lean-to, cut the cinches,' I said to Ring as he began to move away. 'Maybe some bareback riding will take some of the starch out of their shorts!'

Ring smiled and stroked his knives lovingly before disappearing among the trees. The man was good, I'll give him that. One moment he was there, and the next he was gone. Although I had my doubts about his motives and intentions, I had to admit that Ring could be the difference I'd need to repossess the gold. He was a sharp man, I knew, as I had been watching him from day one. And just last night in the clearing, Ring had killed Everson Banks as slick as a whistle, and Everson was known as a badman, and certainly no tenderfoot with a gun. Ring, on the other hand, was a knife man, but from somewhere on his person he had shucked a pistol and as smooth as bear grease on a wax candle, had sent Everson Banks straight to hell. Come what may in the end, I was glad to have Ring on my side right now.

As Ring made his way toward the lean-to, I eased around the side of the cabin opposite of him. Another window on this side was boarded up, allowing me to pass by without peril. And just at the edge of the cabin was a jumble of bushes and vines about waist high. I crouched behind these, gun in hand, and waited for Ring to start the festivities.

Only a few minutes passed and then came the sound of large bodies crashing together, a pole hitting the ground with a dull clatter, and the cluck-clucking of horses' hoofs in soft ground. A wild yell preceded this, then a gunshot shattered the tranquility of the tiny clearing and horses scattered in every direction.

From within the cabin bedlam broke loose as men scrambled out the door, leaving falling chairs and kicked over gear in their wake. Surprisingly, Antoinette was the first one out the door, closely followed by Caxton Banks. As the rest of the occupants spilled into the yard, they spread out, advancing on the lean-to with guns drawn. Even Antoinette followed them, joined by Frank Banks as he brought up the rear.

Quickly I stepped around the corner of the cabin and through the door. Its dusky interior was lit only by the light of the breakfast fire. There were no rooms inside, and gear and bedrolls lay strewn against the walls and in the far corners. Desperately I searched among these, kicking blankets and bedrolls out of the way as I went. From outside I could still hear voices yelling and men stomping about. A few gunshots rang out at random, and I quickened my search.

In the farthest, darkest corner, a rifle lay propped against a blanket roll, and as I grabbed it up and kicked the blanket aside, Antoinette's valise was exposed. My heart skipped a beat and I grabbed the handles excitedly and lifted. It was heavy, very heavy, and I needed not to look to know what was inside. It was the gold, and it was time to make tracks!

As I gathered the valise and turned to leave, the wall next to my face exploded, and my face was sprayed with hot slivers of fire. I wheeled around in fright and fired at a shadowy figure in the doorway, then fired again through the smoke that now hung over the threshold.

Return fire sought me out in my corner and, still clutching the handles of the valise, I moved toward the boarded up window. If I was trapped in here, I was a dead man. There was no gainsaying that, and in desperation I kicked at the boards that covered the window. One broke in two and fell outside as two more shots came from the doorway, one tugging at my pant leg as I kicked again at the boards.

A shadow fell across the doorway and I turned and fired, my effort rewarded by a grunt of pain. But any elation on my part was short lived, as through the doorway I could see Frank and Everson Banks' rifles pointed toward my corner.

I took two steps back from the window, charged with what momentum I could gain, and launched myself at the window and the remaining boards that blocked me from the outside. I half turned as I dove and my back and shoulder struck the boards as bullets from the rifles of Frank and Caxton splattered everywhere.

Fortunately, the remaining boards gave way and I found myself hurtling through the window. In my right hand I still clutched my pistol, in my left the valise. But in turning and twisting as I flew through the window, a corner of the valise caught in the frame of the window and was wrenched from my hand. I landed safely outside, lighting on my shoulder and rolling to my feet. My Colt was still in my hand, but of the valise, only a single handle remained; the rest lost to the interior of the cabin. I cursed my luck bitterly, but now was not the time to wallow in self-pity.

Without breaking stride I ran for the woods, more shots winging past me as I dodged among the trees, first running one way and then another, zigzagging in an effort to throw off the aim of my pursuers.

Blindly, I crashed through the woods, leaping over fallen trees and dodging behind every tree I passed. Once I paused to snap a shot at my pursuers, but could spot no one. Somehow the pursuit had ranged to my left, in the opposite direction of where Ring and I had hidden the horses.

A voice called out here and there, but no more shots were fired. Doggedly, I continued on to the horses, my breath coming in great gasps, and at last I came up to Star and Ring's horse, both with ears pricked forward, moving nervously about at my approach.

It wasn't until I had draped my arms around Star's neck and drawn at least twenty deep, grateful breaths that I realized my left hand still clutched the single handle to the valise. Once again, I cursed my luck and threw the handle into the brush, disgustedly. But even still, I could not brood over the fortunes of fate. Ring was still out there, and with the woods full of Banks' men, and four more returning shortly, we would both need our horses if we were to get out of here alive.

Ring would be swinging back toward me, and I must wait for his return. Since the Bankses at the cabin would be horseless, at least for the time being, any prolonged pursuit would be delayed in forming. But once the horses were gathered up and the four outriders had returned, these woods would be turned upside down in their search for us.

I had wounded someone at the cabin. Who I couldn't say, but with any luck, he would be out of action. Still, seven to two was long odds, and if Ring didn't get back soon, it would be seven to one.

Three hours I waited and nary a sign of Ring. I was worried now. Really worried, as he should have been back long ago. Finally, I could wait no longer. He could be out there wounded, waiting for me to find him, and I could do him no good here. If he was hurt, he would need me now. How I could possibly find him I had no idea, but I had to do something – I had to try. I couldn't just sit here and hope that he would show up.

So admitting, I threw a lead rope on Ring's horse and mounted Star. We moved gingerly through the woods, in a north-eastward arc that would take me around the cabin and in the direction the scattered horses had fled.

Staying far away from the cabin, I circled about, stopping frequently to listen. But only once did I hear anything, and that was a voice, faint and far away, back in the direction of the cabin.

Soon, midday came and passed and still no sign of Ring. I did hear a body of men, probably four or five in number, but I passed wide around them and they noticed me not.

By now I had circled completely around the cabin, rejoining our trail from this morning. No sign. No sound. Nothing. It was as if Ring had simply vanished. To search further than the arc I had taken would take me into the swamps and bayous themselves, and without a boat or canoe, I'd do no good searching there.

Then a thought hit me, and it was the only thing that made sense, excluding the possibility that Ring had been killed near the cabin and that his body was there. The only area I had not searched was a small patch of woods that I had skirted around when I had heard the group of horsemen. They had ridden directly through those woods, and if Ring had been there they would have found him themselves.

But I had heard no shots, no sound of a struggle, and I was close enough to have heard one had one occurred.

But what if? What if they had already found Ring and were taking him back to the cabin when I had heard their passing? What if he was a prisoner even then, his hands and feet tied, his mouth gagged? If they had killed him, there would be no reason to take his body back to the cabin. They would have stripped him of all valuables and left him where he lay. But if he were still alive, and if anyone had thought to take him to Frank for questioning, then Ring could have very well been in their custody as they passed me by.

I could think of nothing else, and even this possibility was far from certain. But it was possible enough that I had to follow up. I couldn't just leave Ring on his own. It was I who had brought him into this, although he had come willingly enough, and I would stick by him until I found him. If he was in fact a prisoner, I would do all I could to free him, and if he were dead, I would give him the burial he deserved.

But for now at least, there wasn't much I could do. Dusk was approaching and soon it would be dark. Any attempt at rescue would have to wait until the morning. As much as I hated to do it, I needed to return to Old Man Carboneau. He knew these woods better than anyone, and if I could get him to help me, perhaps I would have a fighting chance again. How I could do that without endangering Toby I didn't know, but Carboneau was a tough old man and nobody's fool. He'd been up the creek and over the mountain, and more than once. I must find him and right away.

But of course I didn't. He found me. He and Toby. Toby with the smile on her pretty face!

CHAPTER TWELVE

Safe back at Carboneau's cabin, I decided to tell him about the gold. It didn't seem fair to endanger his life and that of Toby's as well, without their full knowledge of everything that was involved. Men would do more than kill for gold, and I felt they should know the full extent of desperation that these men may reach.

I then told him of today's events. He agreed that Ring may have been captured and that even now could be suffering interrogation and rough treatment at the hands of the Bankses. I could see that Carboneau was concerned that Ring may let slip his own presence and thus endanger himself as well as Toby.

I personally felt that Frank Banks would only be interested in me and how most quickly to locate and kill me. But it was possible that in so questioning Ring, if he were in fact held captive, Carboneau and his granddaughter's refuge might come to light.

If so, then they would both be in danger. Frank would want no witnesses left behind that could implicate him in anything shady or nefarious, let alone murder. I too was concerned for Old Man Carboneau and Toby, and asked if there was any other place they could go until this was over.

'I have a trapping shack in the bayous,' Henry Carboneau

replied. 'Use it from time to time when I get tired of dry ground.' He cackled happily and spit a stream of plug tobacco across the stoop. Hitching up his pants, he turned to face me. 'We leave our horses here on dry land. They don't drift far. The water's good here and the grass even better. 'Sides, this is their home. Both of 'em were born in that stable over there.'

He motioned with his head toward the stable where Star stood at a slat trough eating some of Carboneau's precious grain.

'Don't know 'bout your'n, though. Most likely get stole, fine a horse as that Star is.'

'I'm not looking for a place for myself, nor my horse. I just want you and Toby to be out of harm's way. That's a bad bunch I'm after, old man. They'd as soon kill a man as look at him, and with that much money at stake, they'd commence to killing each other.'

I sat down outside on the stoop and leaned back against the cabin. Old Man Carboneau sat on a stump next to me and soon we both had a plate of red beans and rice with large chunks of steaming meat.

I ate hungrily and used my chunk of bread to sop up the juice. Toby ate inside, affording myself and her grandpa the opportunity to discuss matters in private.

'Damn good cook, she is!' Carboneau said, nodding over his shoulder at Toby. 'That's possum meat, son,' he said, smiling. 'Tastes mighty good the way she makes it, but even so, can't claim it as my favorite. Looks too much like a darned old rat to me.' He cackled again and stuffed his mouth with another bite.

If he was looking to make me squeamish, he was wasting his time. I had eaten possum before and it tasted fine to me. When I was a boy, we had eaten about anything a body could catch. When times were hard, one did what one could and thought nothing of it. This was a fine meal, and I was glad to have it. I told Toby so, and she thanked me kindly.

Joining us outside, she sat by her grandpa's knee, her legs folded beneath her, her hands folded neatly in her lap. A stray wisp of hair wafted across her forehead and she shook her head absently, chasing the stray wisp back home.

She was a strikingly pretty girl, but small; yet I found that appealing. There was a peace about her, a sense of tranquility that was refreshing. It had been a long trail for me; first up from Texas to the railheads, then the trip from Abilene to New Orleans. The duel with André Bontemps, and now here in the swamps with my only ally missing – perhaps dead – sharing a meal with an old man and a waif of a girl. I was tired, I suddenly realized. Awfully tired. I would like to sleep for a week. In a bed. A four-poster bed, with sheets and a pillow, only waking to eat and then sleep again.

I must have been staring at Toby, for she smiled sweetly and asked, 'What are you thinking, Dot? You seem so far away.'

I reflected momentarily on her question, forming an answer in my mind before I put it into words. I had talked to girls before around town from time to time, and on a few occasions at railheads. But I had never sparked a girl. The only other girl I had taken a shine to was Antoinette, and that had cost me dearly. But Toby seemed different. Something within her compelled a feeling of trust. I wanted to share with her and get to know her, but most of all, I wanted to make sure that she was safe and that she paid no penalty for my intrusion into her world.

'I was thinking about how nice it is here. How peaceful,' I replied to her question. 'Good company, good food. It's a pleasant furlough from the last few months of my life. I feel as if I could sit here forever, content just to be at peace.' I shifted my position slightly to face her better. 'There's a lot of people in Texas whose very existence depends on my recovering the stolen gold. Without it, they'll all go belly-up. Busted! Those who have land will see the bank's foreclosure, those who can sell, will, but cash money is scarce, as times are hard and money is hard to come by. Many lives are hanging in the balance, here. I only hope I won't let them down.'

She stood up and stretched her legs, resting her hand on her grandfather's shoulder.

'You won't let them down, Dot. You're not that kind of man. Somehow, you'll find a way. I've heard Grandpa say many times, "There's no stopping a man who knows he's right and keeps on coming!" '

Her confidence boosted me, and I only hoped she was right. Tomorrow was another day, for sure, and come hell or high water, things were going to bust open. I felt it in my heart, and I would be ready. God help those who weren't.

Carboneau and Toby packed all the belongings they would need and together we followed a path known only to Carboneau. It led us into the bayous and when we could go no further on horseback, the old man dismounted and began to unload their meagre possessions from the back of Ring's horse.

From beneath a pile of brush and dead branches twenty feet away, Carboneau hauled a canoe and a long pole over to the water and began to load their things into it. When he was done, he turned the horses loose and they wandered only a few paces before they began to graze.

We had decided last night that Carboneau would accompany me while Toby delivered their things to their bayou shack. She would wait there until it was safe to return.

She hugged her grandfather goodbye and placed a kiss on his whiskered face. Taking my hand, she looked into my eyes.

'Be careful, Dot. Don't let anything happen to either of you. I'll be waiting for you both.'

With that, she squeezed my hand and climbed into the canoe, taking the pole in hand and pushing off. We watched her until she had slipped behind a cypress tree and was lost to sight, and then we mounted.

The old man led the way and I fell in behind him. He knew what he was doing and where he was going and he set a pace that was steady and persistent. We covered ground and lots of it, and soon we had rejoined the trail made by Ring and I just yesterday.

The land here now became more woodland than marsh, and we moved slower and more cautiously as our range of vision decreased. It only made sense that Frank and Caxton would have scouts, especially if they had captured Ring and were anticipating any type of rescue on our part.

Leery of such sentinels, Carboneau utilized every bit of cover possible and I followed his lead. Deeper and deeper we stole into the woods, closing ever so surely on the thicket that I had skirted yesterday when I had heard men coming. Carboneau was cutting for sign, his eyes scanning the ground we traversed, searching for any sign that others had gone before. We passed beneath magnolias, pines and oaks, their limbs cloaked in the ever-present Spanish moss. In places, our horses' hoofs stuck in the ground, making a sucking noise as they were withdrawn, and I feared that our advance would be heard in spite of our attempts at stealth.

Honeysuckle flourished in the undergrowth, and azaleas and camellias peeked their multi-coloured petals from amongst the foliage, and once again I was enchanted by the beauty of the bayou marshland.

Quail were abundant and their sudden bursts from cover more than once startled me to the point of making my heart race. Doves sped by overhead and if one listened close, turkeys could be heard gobbling in the far distant clearings. I could see how Toby and Old Man Carboneau lived well, as the bounty of the land was abundantly evident. At their hut I had seen the skins of raccoons, muskrats, minks and a wildcat's, as well as the head of a huge wild hog with its razor sharp tusks curving menacingly from a snarling mouth.

The creeks and sloughs were full of crayfish, the deeper water with bass, perch, catfish and a fish Toby had called a gaspergou. It was a bountiful land, no doubt about it.

It seemed a shame to me that men's greed would cause such a haven to be marred by the blood and death of one another. Men had already died here, and perhaps my companion, Ring. Others would soon die, of that there was no doubt. But the land would live on. The trees, the birds, the fish and animals, each ignoring the bones of the dead men left behind. Left behind by man's greed.

Ahead, Carboneau pulled up and motioned me forward. As I drew abreast of him, I looked to where he was pointing. Clearly visible in the soft earth were the hoof prints of four horses, closely bunched and pointed at the thicket that loomed to the immediate east.

Last night Carboneau had attempted to explain our exact location to me. We were east of New Orleans and only a few miles from Lake Borgne. North of us was Lake Pontchartrain, and to the south of us, the meandering Mississippi; an area of approximately fifty square miles, large enough to hide in, yet small enough to die in.

The thicket we were now approaching was to our east. Toby was somewhere to our south and hopefully by now safely settled in the bayou shack. The smuggler's cabin where I had almost recovered the gold was north of us by a few miles, and somewhere between here and there were the Bankses, Frank and Caxton, and their gunmen, as well as Antoinette.

Cautiously, we followed the tracks of the four riders. They led us straight to the thicket, and almost in the middle of the thicket was a clearing. It was deserted! Not a soul in sight, but men had been here. A fire still smouldered off to one side and tracks were everywhere, both of man and beast.

Carboneau cast about, as did I, each of us reading the tale that was written on the earth. At the foot of one tree, we could both see that someone had sat with his back against the trunk of the tree. His leg and heel marks were plain to see. The far side of the tree trunk showed signs of scuffing and it was evident that someone had been tied here, proba- bly overnight. Unless there was someone around that I was not aware of, it had to be Ring, and he was still alive.

We scouted about a while longer and finally determined that this camp had been vacated at early dawn. We extin- guished the fire completely before taking the trail again. The tracks were easy to follow, striking east for a mile or so where they were joined by others. Six more horses had joined the four from the clearing, two of these being led – more than likely the horses of Everson Banks and the man from the bar in Abilene, both of whom had been killed in the fight where Antoinette had shot me.

One of these was mounted, probably by Ring. But instead of turning north toward the smuggler's cabin, they struck south in the direction Carboneau and I had just came that morning and where Toby now awaited our return.

Ring could not possibly know about the cabin in the bayous. Its existence had only been revealed last night by Carboneau, so if he had been forced to talk, he couldn't have disclosed its location to the Bankses. But he did know about the cabin where we had stayed the night with Carboneau and Toby, and if they planned to flank us and take us from behind, this southerly pitch would be necessary to attack us from arrears. We discussed this very possibility,

Carboneau and I, and agreed that it made sense.

The Bankses would need to go south until they struck the bayous, then turn west and follow its fringe until they obtained a southern position below the hut. Then they could strike north until they closed upon the hut. Carboneau estimated that such a journey would bring them to the hut, at best, shortly after sunset. That cover of darkness would provide the best opportunity to scout the hut and either plan an attack against us or carry one out. It was a good plan, but one that had an essential flaw: The hut was deserted, and we were now behind them.

Agreeing that there would be no danger to Toby, we decided to follow at a safe distance, knowing that Ring would be left behind if any attack on us was effected. They would probably leave a guard or two with him to keep him quiet and out of the way. Perhaps then we could wrest him away from their custody.

And what of the gold? I felt sure that Frank would not let it out of his sight, so if a strike against us did in fact take place, or at least against where they thought us to be, I believed Frank would stay with the gold and Ring. With them surely would be Antoinette, and perhaps one other gunman. I doubted that we would ever have better odds, but exactly how much I could depend on Carboneau I didn't know. His first obligation was to Toby and if it got hot and heavy, I wouldn't blame him if he cut and ran.

The only sure bet I had was myself. I had to recover the gold. There was no other option, nor any other obligation. Carboneau had done his job and once we had caught up with the Bankses, I would send him on his way. Toby needed him more than me, and alone I could move faster and more certainly without the responsibility of another person on my mind.

Timing would be essential and we must come upon the

Bankses once they had already made camp. I felt sure that they would attack us tonight, as Frank wanted me dead beyond anything else. He would send an advance party, most likely led by Caxton. Once they were gone, that would be the time for my own assault and even though I would be outnumbered by at least three guns, counting Antoinette, the surprise my appearance would make should be enough to even the odds. The kicker, once again, was Antoinette.

'Don't you worry about the young lady,' Carboneau said. 'I'll take care of her for you.'

'I don't want her hurt, old man, even though she may deserve it.'

Carboneau cackled dryly and said, 'She won't be hurt, son. Just leave her to me. If there's a better Injun in these parts, I've never met him.'

I contemplated a moment on his words. I would prefer that Carboneau return to Toby, but Antoinette was a problem. She had proven herself dangerous and I didn't need a woman jumping up in the middle of a gun battle, blasting away at me. But at my question, Carboneau explained his intentions to me and I smiled, then laughed; my first good laugh in quite a while.

We found their camp easy, as their fire was a beacon a blind man could see. They had chosen a good spot about two miles from Carboneau's hut and beneath a rise in the land that would block their campsite from any eyes at the hut. The only flaw in their strategy, of course, was that the hut was vacated.

Once we were sure of their location, we pulled back and made a cold camp of our own. We watered the horses in a slough then hobbled both in a nice patch of grass where they hastily began to feed.

We waited an hour or so until the sun was long set, then tied our horses securely to a sound tree. Carboneau had cleaned and double-checked his rifle and was now anxious to be off. For an old man, he was mighty spry and was weathering this intrusion into his world rather well – almost as if he was enjoying himself.

Me? I found no pleasure in any of this, only an abiding desire to be done with it and on my way back to Texas with the gold. By now, Slim Hite and Gunner Walls would have returned to Texas, and the ranchers who had invested all they had in this cattle drive would be worried sick, knowing that their very livelihoods rested in my hands, and in a battle that they had no control over.

If I were to fail I would be blamed, and rightly so.

Not far ahead lay the camp of the men who had stolen the gold – and the gold was there for the taking. Even outnumbered as I was, a fast gun and a fast mind could win the day. I was fast. Believe me, I knew I was fast. But was I fast enough to win against so many dangerous gunmen? There was a reckoning coming, and it was coming fast.

With that thought in mind, I stood up and checked my pistol one last time, as well as my rifle. Carboneau looked expectantly at me and I nodded.

'Lead on, old man, let's get the ball rolling!'

He moved like a ghost, that old man did, and I was right on his tail. It was completely dark now, with only a slight slice of moon in the sky. Somewhere in the distance a wildcat screamed, and just overhead an owl screeched and sped away on frantic wings. The night creatures and insects filled the night with their croaks and cries, our passage seeming to disturb them not at all.

When the campfire came into sight again, Carboneau slowed his pace and the last few hundred yards were covered as silently as possible. Carboneau put me in a perfect position both to watch and listen, and I could clearly see Ring. He was tied to a tree on the far side of the camp. Antoinette leaned against a tree near him, and Frank Banks stood in the middle of camp. Caxton was next to him and together they stood facing their hired gunmen who were listening closely as Frank spoke.

Sawyer Bates and Hondo Cain each kneeled across the fire from Frank, a cup of coffee in their hands, and of the other three gunmen, I only recognized one, and he was Corbin White from the Brazos Country in Texas. The other two were unknown to me, but they were loaded for bear, and neither one would be a man to fool with.

From my place behind an old magnolia covered in moss, I listened as Frank gave his orders.

'When you get there, surround the hut first. I don't want anyone to get away. Kill every damn one of them; the old man, the girl, and most especially Dot Pickett. When he's dead, bring his body back. I want to see it in person. Don't waste any time tomfooling around with that girl, either. Kill 'em all and get Pickett's body back here as fast as you can.'

Sawyer Bates stood up and tossed the dregs from his cup into the fire. 'What about him?' he said, nodding toward Ring. 'Want I should kill him now?'

Ring looked up at Frank and I could see his face was a mess. He had been beaten badly, and I only noticed now that his feet were bare. The soles of his feet were black and even at this distance I could see that they were swollen, that they had been burned. His face and shirt were covered with blood and as he squinted to look at Frank, he winced in obvious pain.

'No,' Frank answered, studying Ring with ill concealed contempt. 'If they're not where he said they'd be, we'll make him talk some more.'

Ring dropped his gaze from Frank, staring mutely at the ground between his legs.

'Tillman, you're staying here with me. The rest of you

know the plan. Move out with Caxton and let's get this over.'

As the men began to rise in response to his orders, Frank added one last thing. 'Men, this man killed my sons. All three of them. I've waited a long time for this day. I want him dead, by God, and no excuses. You've one simple task to carry out and we're off to California. Don't mess this up, boys, and I mean it!'

'Don't you worry, Uncle Frank,' Caxton said. 'I've waited for this day as long as you. If he's there, he's a dead man, I personally guarantee you that!'

With that, they moved to their horses and mounted up, Caxton Banks leading the way.

I searched the camp for the gold, my eyes seeking every hiding place possible. A picket rope had been stretched between two oak trees and near one horse was a pile of gear. I thought I could just make out the shape of a valise, but I couldn't be sure. A saddle blanket hid most of it from my view, but there was nothing else that I could see that could be the gold.

I watched Frank as he moved to the fire and poured himself a cup of coffee. He approached Ring then and cold-heartedly kicked his tortured feet.

'Things better be as you said, Cajun Boy, or you'll get a real taste of pain.'

Frank Banks kicked Ring's feet again, but Ring only gritted his teeth and ignored him.

Turning, he sauntered casually back to the fire and as I watched him, a loathing I had never felt for any man came over me. I had killed his sons, that was true, but they had come asking for it and had gotten what they deserved. But from all I had heard, it was Frank Banks who had pushed his sons into outlawry and murder. It was he who taught them to steal and cheat. Their deaths were his fault as much as mine, if not more so. The apple doesn't fall far from the tree, they say, and Frank Banks was the tree that bore the fruit of his evil family.

And what about Antoinette? What impression had he had on her life? Frank had married her mother and Antoinette had been young and at the mercy of his tyranny. How much of an effect had he had on her? Had his cruelness and meanness shaped her into something she otherwise might not have become? Frank Banks was an evil man, of that there was no doubt.

I was tempted to raise my rifle and kill him where he stood, without warning, as he surely would have done to me. But in spite of my disdain for the man and all that he stood for, I couldn't just shoot him out of hand. That was too close to murder. But believe you me, Frank Banks was a marked man, and he would be the first one I sent to hell when the chance presented itself.

Frank moved over near the pile of gear that I believed held the gold, and Antoinette followed him, taking a seat on a blanket and crossing her legs beneath her.

They talked quietly there amongst themselves, their words unclear to my ears. It was getting close to the time where I would have to make a move one way or the other, as at any moment now Caxton Banks should discover that the hut was empty. Once they did, they would come immediately back to this camp and my chance would be lost.

At that moment, Antoinette rose and excused herself from Frank, making her way off into the trees and away from camp. Carboneau, who had sat silently by my side, now rose nimbly and disappeared into the woods. The man called Tillman, who had stayed behind with Frank to help guard Ring, lay sprawled beneath a tree near Ring's, his hat pulled over his face and apparently asleep.

Leaving my place behind the old magnolia, I moved around the camp in the opposite direction from Carboneau.

I was not as good in the woods as he, but nevertheless my movement went undetected. Soon I was behind the tree that towered above Ring and I was only five feet or so away from him when Tillman stood up and stretched, making his way to the coffeepot.

Now was my chance and I moved quickly to Ring and touched his shoulder. Instantly he was alert, but he kept his head down and gave no sign of recognition. Taking my knife from my pocket, I opened the clasp silently and began to cut at the ropes that held him to the tree.

From the looks of his feet, I'd have to carry him, and I hadn't planned on that. Somehow I'd hoped to slip in and wrest the gold from camp, killing whoever was in my way, while Carboneau took care of Antoinette. How I would do that now with Ring in the condition he was, I didn't know. But it was clear that first of all I must get Ring safely away from camp. But I couldn't carry him all the way to the horses, not and still have a chance to come back for the gold.

His ropes were loose now and his hands were free. Yet still he didn't move. He knew that to do so now would give my presence away.

Just as I was about to give up on discovering a way to get Ring out of camp without getting us both shot, a muffled shriek sounded from the other side of camp off in the woods where Antoinette had disappeared. Tillman dropped his cup of coffee and drew his pistol. Frank did likewise, his hand motioning at Tillman to stay put.

Taking a chance, I stepped around the tree and scooped Ring into my arms, and before you could say 'scat', I faded into the woods with my friend in tow. The ground around the tree had been free of limbs and soft underfoot, and our exit had gone undetected.

I had travelled a good one hundred yards from the camp

before I heard Frank's angry yell: 'The Cajun, damn it! The Cajun's gone!'

I sat Ring down and handed him my extra pistol, telling him to wait where he was. He nodded and I struck out for the camp again, returning by a slightly different route.

When I arrived, no one was there. It was empty, and not a sound came from the surrounding woods. My eyes sought out the pile of gear and it was still there, seemingly untouched or moved from when I had last observed.

Following the edge of the camp, I skirted around to the picket line where the horses stood placidly. One rolled his eyes at me as I approached and I spoke gently to him and stroked his neck.

Looking about I could see no one, nor did I hear anything. It was as if everyone had dropped off the face of the earth.

Shifting my drawn pistol to my left hand, I reached to my right and lifted the blanket. Sure enough, underneath was the valise, its one handle missing, the other drooping sadly on one side. I took a deep breath and let it out, my right hand closing over the handle. As I began to lift the valise, Frank Banks stepped from behind the tree that I had thought incapable of hiding a man, but the shadow from one of the horses had blocked my view and the light from the moon had been too weak to reveal Frank's hiding place. He had positioned himself well, and I was fairly caught.

'Don't try it, Pickett,' he half spat at me. 'You freeze, you son of a bitch, or I'll blow your damned head off.'

I moved not an inch, freezing as he had ordered, my right hand holding the handle of the valise. My left hand still held my pistol, but in reaching for the valise, my left hand had naturally gone slightly behind my back and hip, hiding the pistol from his view. Frank knew that I was right handed, and that I carried only one gun on my right side. He had seen this in Abilene. That holster on my right side was empty, but my right arm blocked his view and with the poor light of the moon, he could not see that my holster was empty. Frank Banks thought he had caught me unarmed, with my hand in the cookie jar. He couldn't see the pistol in my left hand, nor could he possibly know that I was almost as good with my left hand as with my right. If I could just get him to step a little closer, clearing his body from the tree that still shielded him from my left arm, I just might be able to get off a shot.

'All right, Frank, I give up. You've got me dead to rights.'

He leaned slightly forward, his gun hand steady and unwavering, the solitary eye of his pistol boring a hole in my forehead.

'You're damn right I do,' he exclaimed, his voice high-pitched with excitement. 'I knew it was you and I knew you'd come for the gold.'

He was still too far behind the tree and within the shadow of darkness it cast. I couldn't risk a shot as I would only get one. He could fire at any time and if he did, I was dead. But his hate was so strong that just killing me wasn't enough. He had to crow over me and let me know what he was going to do.

'You're just a snot-nosed kid, Pickett, and my boys are dead because of you. How you killed them I'll never know. You're sure not the gunman I thought you were. How does it feel, Pickett? Did my sons feel this way? Did you even give them a chance?'

'They had their chance, Frank, more chance than they ever gave anyone.'

I moved a bit in an effort to relieve the stress on my back.

'Don't try it, Pickett. You'll never make it.'

I could see the smirk on his face and when I took my chance, I knew exactly where my shot would go: Right in the middle of his smirk.

'I'm not moving, Frank. Just a bit uncomfortable like this. You want me to toss you the gold?'

'It's fine where it is. Don't try any tricks.'

I looked from him to the bag, then back to him again. 'It seems light, Frank. Someone been raiding the bag?' Come on, you bastard, I thought to myself. Just a little closer. 'When was the last time you checked this bag?'

'What do you mean, Pickett? What are you talking about?'

I could hear the doubt that had crept into his voice and I spurred him even harder.

'Why, this bag is empty. Caxton's not coming back. He's left with your gold.'

That was all it took as he stepped forward to see better, bringing his entire body into view, his pistol dropping slightly.

Instantly, I raised up and whipped my left arm around, my finger closing on the trigger and firing a round point blank into his face. He got off a shot, but it was too late, his bullet plowing a furrow in the earth next to the valise even as his dead body hit the ground.

CHAPTER THIRTEEN

Carboneau had accomplished his mission, catching Antoinette away from camp on a call of nature. He had roped her and hogtied her, stuffing a rag in her mouth and a kerchief around that, so she couldn't spit it out. He had left her like that, trussed up like a hog going to slaughter, beneath an oak tree fifty yards from camp.

On his way back to camp he had spotted Tillman slinking about in the woods looking for Antoinette. Somehow he had conked him on the head, rendering him unconscious.

Gathering up the gold, we put both Antoinette and Tillman on a horse, mounted two ourselves and cut the last one loose. The gold I carried with me, and it would not leave my sight again.

We lit a shuck out of camp as Caxton and his men would be returning at any time. Ring was waiting for us where I had left him and once again reunited, we made for our own horses.

I mounted Star and cut the horse from the camp loose. After we were all remounted on our own horses we lit out once again, determined to leave this part of the marshland far behind.

Carboneau was anxious to join Toby at the bayou shack,

and I decided to go with him. Ring needed medical attention and Toby could help with that, but what was I to do with Antoinette and Tillman?

If I let them go they would unite with Caxton and tell them of the bayou shack. That would endanger everyone anew, and that I couldn't afford. Now that the gold had been recovered I wanted to sit on it at the bayou shack. You could be sure that Caxton wouldn't give up now, not since the gold was back in my hands. He would search every inch of this marshland. But if the bayou shack was as hidden and inaccessible as Carboneau said, they would never find us there. All I had to do was wait until Caxton at last gave up, or assumed that I had given him the slip, and left to pursue me elsewhere. But this I couldn't do with both Tillman and Antoinette in tow. I would have to do something about them, and soon, as we would shortly be at the edge of the bayou where Toby had left us in the canoe.

Another problem was how we would get to the shack. Toby had left in the canoe and we had no way to let her know that we intended to join her at her bayou refuge. But at my question to Carboneau, he only smiled and said there would be no problem.

Our two prisoners rode in silence, Antoinette still gagged and Tillman content to remain unnoticed. When we finally reached the glade where Carboneau had secreted the canoe, I helped Antoinette down from her mount. When she stumbled, Carboneau caught her arm and helped her to sit on the damp, soft ground.

Ring was next, and he stepped gingerly on his feet, barely able to support any weight. When he was seated close to Antoinette, I hauled Tillman from the saddle. His hands were still bound behind his back, but he landed on his feet easily.

'Stretch your legs a bit if you want,' I said to him. 'It's

going to be. . . .'

Before I could finish the sentence, a shot rang out behind me, closely followed by another. Tillman's head jerked violently and he fell face-first to the ground. I snapped around furiously, drawing my pistol as I did. Ring had risen to his knees and from that position had fired the two shots at Tillman.

'What the hell are you doing?' I roared at him, my eyes moving from him to Tillman.

Ring ignored me but lowered his pistol. It was the extra gun I had given him earlier that night. As he tossed it aside I hurried to Tillman, and with the toe of my boot rolled his body over. His eyes were dead and unseeing.

Returning to Ring, I challenged him angrily.

'What is wrong with you?! That was cold blooded murder!' He looked up at me, a vacant look in his eyes. 'That man's hands were tied behind his back!' I said.

'So were mine,' Ring answered coldly, looking at the lifeless form of Tillman's body. 'So were mine while he burned my feet.' He looked over at Antoinette, his face cloudy with pain and anger. 'She's lucky she's not next to him. It was her idea in the first place.'

I looked at Antoinette and she lowered her eyes quickly, but not before I saw the guilt and fear in them.

I shook my head and turned away from her, walking back to the body of Tillman. 'Live by the sword, die by the sword,' I mused. But it was a hell of a way to go.

Looking over my shoulder, I said to Carboneau, 'Let's get rid of the body. Push him off in the water.'

I grabbed his feet and the old man his shoulders, and together we half pulled, half rolled him in the water. Slowly he disappeared under the surface, and ever so gently began to slip from sight.

'Don't fret, son,' Carboneau said. 'Gators'll get him. Be

the best damn contribution he ever made in this world.'

With that, he cackled and called over his shoulder. 'Wait for me here. I'll be back shortly.'

I watched silently as he disappeared in the darkness. When he was gone I went to Antoinette and removed her gag. Ring was reclining on his side, his feet obviously causing him great pain.

'Would you like a drink?' I inquired of her.

She only nodded, and I removed the canteen from my saddle, lifting her chin with my hand as I helped her drink. When she was through, she used her shoulder to wipe her mouth and questioningly looked up at me.

'What do you plan to do with me?'

I stood slowly, screwing the top back on to the canteen as she awaited my reply.

Squinting my face as if deep in thought, I paused a moment before using my head to motion toward the spot where Tillman's body had been disposed. Her eyes flew open and she looked at me with horror.

'You wouldn't dare!' she said indignantly, squirming beneath my glare.

'Try me!' I replied. 'Just one peep out of you and we'll see how good you can swim!'

Turning away from her, I went to Ring. He was in great pain, but he bore it solemnly. I asked him if there was anything I could do for him and he only shook his head. I squeezed his shoulder in what I hoped to be a heartening gesture.

'We're taking you to Toby,' I told him reassuringly. 'She'll take care of you. A little rest, some good vittles and you'll be like new.'

He tried to smile in response, but it looked more like a grimace, his eyes closing painfully with the effort.

I left him be and checked the horses. Antoinette was as

quiet as a church mouse, but I could feel her eyes following my every move. I could find in my heart no sympathy for her. She was grown and she had known what she was getting into. She had made her choices with her own free will and she, like men and women everywhere, must pay the price for her actions. Granted, I would never throw her to the fishes, but as long as she thought I might, she would be a lot easier to handle.

Just as I began to wonder about Carboneau, the muffled sound of an oar striking a gunwale came across the bayou. It was a distinctive sound, one you never forgot, even if you weren't a seafarer. As if to prove me right, the nose of a flat-boat crept into sight, Carboneau pulling the oars gently, his back turned toward us. Glancing over his shoulder, he guided the boat to dry land and nimbly debarked to face me on the bank.

He grinned his toothless smile at me and I asked, 'Just how many boats you got hidden around here?'

He slapped his thigh and cackled, 'A whole damn fleet, son! Don't you know an old pirate when you see one?'

There was probably more truth to that than I cared to admit, but I lay off at being thankful at his providence. My success in recovering the gold was in large part due to him and my capacity to keep it and get away with it would be, as well. Carboneau was a good man to have around, and his age was not the deterrent that he would have you believe. He got around on foot in these woods a lot better than I did – and in the water? Well, he was the pirate, not I!

We began to load our gear into the flatboat, and I cautiously sat the gold in the middle with our saddles surrounding it. Antoinette came next, and although I expected her to complain or cajole, she held her tongue. I believe that, at least for now, she was content to go where the gold went.

I was hesitant about turning the horses loose. When Caxton Banks was unable to find us immediately, he would start a search and eventually that search would turn up the horses. That would serve to defeat us in two ways: Once he found the horses, especially my horse Star, he would know that we had taken to the water. Secondly, I would be giving up the very transportation that I would need to eventually convey the gold safely out of here. Star was a good horse, too, about the best I had ever had.

'Old man, are you sure there's no way to take the horses with us?' I inquired hopefully. 'Some way we can get them to the shack?'

He hitched his pants up and looked at me ruefully. 'Never said there weren't no way, son.'

'I thought you said that you and Toby always turned your horses loose here.'

'That's right, I did. And we do.' He looked at me as if I'd gone stupid. 'That doesn't mean we couldn't take 'em, though, son. Only that it's faster not to.'

I glared at him in exasperation, anxious to be out of here before Caxton and his men showed up.

'So you mean we can?'

'Darn right, we can. Only it'll take some doin'. That's why Toby and I never bother.'

Squatting by the water's edge, he scooped up two hand-fuls of water and splashed it on his face.

'We'll have to wade 'em about a half mile north, then there's a bar of land, runs 'bout a mile east. From there we can swim them across to a shallow, then wade 'em another half mile or so till we come up to a magnolia grove, 'bout a mile from the shack. From there, the water's shallow, never more than a brisket, and we can wade up straight through. 'Round about way to go, but it'll get us there.' He hitched up his pants and looked at me questioningly.

'Let's give her a try then, old man. I can't afford to be without these horses. It's a long walk from here to Texas and I ain't got my walking shoes with me!'

He cackled and nodded his head. 'You know how to row a boat, son?' At my hesitant nod he rolled his eyes and continued. 'You just follow me then. I'll lead the horses and you can come along behind us. Once we hit that bar of land, you can row beside us and we'll be fine. Just keep the nose of the boat pointed where you want to go.' This last part he said with a wry smile on his whiskered face.

'Don't worry about me, old man. I ain't never drownt before. You just lead the way and we'll be right behind you.'

As brave as my words were, it took a while to get the hang of rowing. We had loaded Ring last, with his back resting against the gold, but he was too far out of his head to take notice of my zigzagging start. Antoinette was not, however, and although she kept her mouth shut, her snorts and body movement gave vent to her contempt of my oarsmanship. Nevertheless, I soon had the hang of it and we mirrored Carboneau's every step.

I'll give it to that old man, he was game and he never let up once. When he set his teeth to the bit, he kept a-goin'.

The only rest we took was at the magnolia grove, and she was a short one. I had untied Antoinette's hands so she could stretch, drink and answer a call to nature. I wasn't afraid she'd run, as there was no place to go, but she was welcome to try if she wanted. Serve her right did she leave off and drown.

Around noon, we came in sight of the shack. A wisp of smoke wafted from the flue atop the roof and disappeared in the overhanging limbs of a live oak tree.

The canoe that Toby had employed was turned on its side near the bank. As we drew nigh, her diminutive form appeared from the shadows and my breath caught, as once

139

again I was struck by the innocence and beauty she bespoke. The smile on her face was one of both happiness and relief, and I found my own sentiments to be the same.

As her grandfather led the horses on to what was actually a small island, she pitched in and gave help. There was no corral here or stable, no lean-to or fence; but the water that surrounded this island would act as a barrier, and the lush green grass would abort any temptation to stray. Knowing this, Carboneau simply let the horses loose and they strolled casually off to graze and roll in the dirt near the water's edge.

I nosed the flatboat on to the bank and Toby grabbed hold and helped haul us further ashore. She was staring at Antoinette, and Antoinette was staring right back. You could have cut the animosity with a knife, and a sense of foreboding came over me.

As if it wasn't enough having Caxton Banks and his hired men trying to kill us all, now I would have two women in the same camp wanting to kill each other at the first opportunity. If looks could kill, they would both be dead already.

Toby at last tore her gaze from that of Antoinette's and smiled sweetly at me.

'Hi, Dot! How are you?' As she looked me up and down, I smiled in return.

'I'm fine, Toby. Thanks to your grandfather.'

She looked over her shoulder and smiled adoringly at the old man who was tromping toward us, his rifle still in his gnarled hand.

Her gaze then caught sight of Ring and his bare, burned feet, and she gasped.

'Oh my God! What happened?'

Her hand went to her mouth in shock and I quickly explained what they had done to Ring. Through the entire rendition, her face betrayed her horror and dismay. Here was a girl whose heart was pure and honest, kind and gentle, and she was very rudely being introduced to the reality of the world and the evil men who dwelled within it. She was a trooper, though, I'll give her that, and as soon as my story was over, she was all business.

Carboneau helped Antoinette out of the boat while Toby and I carried Ring inside. She made a bed for him using our saddle blankets covered with a clean blanket, and another blanket for a cover.

She wasted no time attending his poor, blistered feet, but the stench that came from them was too much for me, so I left her on her own. If anyone could bring Ring around, it was her. And I had no doubt that Ring would be up and about before much longer.

When they had called this place a shack, they had been generous. How it was standing was beyond me, and it was in desperate need of repair. Once the flatboat was offloaded of all our gear, I set about repairing the shack as best I could. I hoped that we could stay here for a week or two, out of sight and out of mind. I didn't see any way that Caxton Banks could find us, nor be made aware of our presence. Surely after a couple of weeks at most, he would believe I had somehow given him the slip, perhaps returned to New Orleans or even now was racing to Texas with the gold. Eventually he would have to abandon his search and seek me elsewhere. He also would know that if he waited too long, I would be long gone and forever out of his reach. I believe he would only search for me a few days before moving on. Perhaps he would leave a man or two behind to watch for me, but I didn't believe he would stay long once he lost our trail, and I had made sure that our trail had ended short of the water, our tracks pointing in another direction and disappearing in a thicket of live oak and pines. There was no clue to point him in our true direction, so my plan was to bide our time until the woods had cleared of the rabble who sought to kill us and steal the gold again. When a sufficient time had passed, I would light a shuck to Texas, the gold safe in my care.

Soon, Carboneau joined me and we worked furiously at repairing the shack. We had few tools available, but by the end of the day had done a fair job.

Antoinette had sat on a stump most of the afternoon, but had eventually entered the shack. The gold was inside, next to Ring, but there was nothing she could do with it or any place she could go with it. I was more concerned with Antoinette and Toby, yet no sounds of murder had reached my ears, so Carboneau and I had happily finished our repairs on the shack.

That night we ate ravenously and slept like the dead. But as soon as the sun was up, I was out and about. By mid morning, I was content with the shack and, pronouncing it livable for the next two weeks, had quit my task. Antoinette and Toby seemed to be sharing a silent truce as they worked together in preparing our meals and arranging our sleeping places. As Antoinette moved about, she ignored me completely and I did nothing to improve the status, content to leave well enough alone.

We slipped into a pattern of tranquility and peace. The days passed quietly, finding myself and Carboneau constantly gathering food as we did our best to bring Ring back to health and to provide for everyone within our island sanctuary.

Over the days, I grew to admire and respect Henry Carboneau as much as anyone I had ever known. He was always cheerful, affable and tireless in his pursuit of game and fish. He was a true woodsman, knowing every manner of survival, of hunting and fishing, as well as trapping and living entirely off the land. He knew every creature, every plant and insect that lived, breathed or crawled, and every day that passed he taught me something new or showed me something different. My respect for him grew each day, as well as my curiosity.

He told me that he was born in 1799 and was raised in the little village of Barataria Bay in the Gulf of Mexico. His father was Pierre Carboneau, a Frenchman and friend to Jean Lafitte, a notorious pirate known throughout Louisiana and especially in New Orleans. Pierre had been a sailor with Jean Lafitte and had raided Spanish ships on the high seas. As a boy Henry Carboneau had worshipped his father, and anxiously awaited his return to port to listen rapturously to his tales of piracy, ships and battling for their lives on the open water.

When Henry was fourteen, he had joined his father as a cabin boy and had sailed with Lafitte to England. There, Britain had offered Jean Lafitte a large amount of money and a naval captaincy to betray the United States and assist Britain in an attack against New Orleans. Jean Lafitte had gathered all the information that he could and quickly sailed back to New Orleans, notifying the United States of Britain's plans.

Jean Lafitte, Pierre Carboneau, and his fifteen-year-old son Henry, fought for General Andrew Jackson at New Orleans in the Battle of 1815. It was a bittersweet victory for young Henry. The British had been repulsed and Jean Lafitte was later pardoned by President James Madison. But Henry's father had lost a leg to a cannon ball and later had succumbed to infection and fever. Young Henry buried his father and returned to his seaside village. There he learned of his mother's death. She had sadly died a month earlier, almost to the day that her husband had been wounded.

Now an orphan, young Henry returned to New Orleans and joined Lafitte once again. Things were different now, as

Lafitte had been pardoned and had turned his back on piracy. Henry spent his days on shore finding work where he could, sleeping in the streets most of the time, his belly gaunt from hunger.

When Lafitte decided to move to Galveston, young Henry went with him. There the town of Campeche was established, and for a period of time things went well. But eventually Lafitte grew tired of the domesticity of life in Campeche, and like all good pirates, returned to the high seas. This was a boon to young Henry, who longed for adventure and hand-to-hand combat on the decks of a Spanish galleon.

By the time young Henry was twenty-one years old, he was battle tested and a veteran of pirate raids, smuggling and death on the high seas. But Lafitte's return to piracy had not gone unnoticed, and in 1821 a US force was sent against him. Facing imprisonment or exile, Lafitte had chosen to sail away, his future and his destiny unknown.

Young Henry chose to stay behind, not willing to risk his life to an unknown future and an unknown land. Louisiana was his home and here he would stay.

He went on to tell me a story that hitherto had never been shared with anyone. Not even Toby knew it in its entirety.

In the last days of Lafitte's piracy, a sea chest had been filled with the booty of recent raids. Its destination had been New Orleans where Lafitte had intended to sell the valuables in order to replenish his failing finances. The chest had been sent by boat with two of Lafitte's most trusted lieutenants in command. Lafitte was to follow and meet his lieutenants at the very smuggler's cabin where the Bankses had fled with my gold.

They had never shown, and later Lafitte was furious! A thorough search had resulted in only one clue – a wounded man who had been with the chest. He told of being attacked by cutthroats who had apparently known nothing of the booty. They had simply run into the company of men escorting the chest and had seized the opportunity to rob and commit murder. The two lieutenants had fled by boat with the chest, while the rest of the escorts confronted the cutthroats. The ensuing melee had afforded the lieutenants enough time to flee and they had immediately hidden the chest.

By that time the engagement was over, the entire escort killed by the cutthroats. The more exuberant of the attackers had followed up their assault and killed the two lieutenants, oblivious to the existence of the sea chest entirely. The only survivor was the wounded man, and he had been left for dead.

Somehow, wounded though he was, he had made his way through the woods and bayous and by chance happened upon an abandoned boat. He had climbed aboard, passed out and had later been found.

After telling his story, the wounded man had died. How far he had drifted in the boat had never been determined, so the exact location of the sea chest remained unknown. But its proximity was not secret. The rescuer knew better than any the approximate location of the sea chest with its ingots of gold, emeralds and Spanish medallions.

This rescuer had searched for Jean Lafitte to inform him of what he had discovered, but Lafitte had been afield himself, searching for the chest. And once the rescuer began his own search for the gold, he had become so entranced in its discovery that he had forgotten time. Once he had given up and returned to Campeche, Jean Lafitte was preparing to sail away.

Deeming it now too late, the rescuer had abandoned his mission to report to Lafitte, and by the next day the notorious pirate was gone, never to be seen again in the Gulf of

Mexico. The only question that now remained was who had the rescuer been and what had happened to him. Had he found the chest? Had he been killed? At these questions, Carboneau assured me that the rescuer had not been killed, and that he had never found the chest. I asked him how he could be so sure, and he had simply replied that the rescuer who had found the wounded man and listened to his tale was none other than himself; young Henry Carboneau.

CHAPTER FOURTEEN

Ten days had passed since our retreat to the bayou sanctuary, and nary a peep from anyone, enemy or otherwise. The last two days, Old Man Carboneau and I had expanded our range looking for game so that we could scout for signs at the same time. On each day we found nothing, not a sign, scent or sound, and I believed that our ruse had worked. Caxton Banks could not afford to let me get away. Everything he had schemed and plotted for was tied up in the gold, and did he let it slip away, he would be left with nothing. He had lost a brother and an uncle, and even to a man like Caxton, that might mean more to him than the gold. Until now, the only thing personal between he and I was the gold, but now two more members of his family were dead, and his stepsister was held hostage by myself. If there had been anything Caxton wouldn't have done before to kill me and get the gold, there was definitely nothing now.

Mayhap he was long gone by now, chasing some trail to Texas or searching the streets of New Orleans. But I didn't think so. Until he was sure I had given him the slip, he couldn't chance leaving the last place he'd seen me. He knew the gold was with me and where I went, the gold would be. All he had to do was find me and he'd find the gold.

This marshland covered a large area of land. They could

cut and search for signs forever without finding anything, and as long as we didn't make any, we would be safe. But I couldn't hide here forever. Caxton may have deduced the same and he could have scouts out at strategic intervals just waiting for us to make our escape. We couldn't go east or north, as lakes blocked us in both directions. South of us was the Mississippi and the Gulf of Mexico; we would find no relief there. If Caxton put out sentinels blocking our escape to the west, we would eventually have to come to him. He could sit back and wait, but how long could he wait? How long could I, for that matter?

I knew that the time to do something was at hand. I couldn't wait much longer; to do so would only stall the inevitable and Caxton might even send to New Orleans for reinforcements, if he hadn't done so already. No, it was time to go. There was too much at stake to tarry longer.

Ring was healthy enough to get back to New Orleans. He could take Antoinette with him. They had spent a lot of time talking lately anyway, and it was making me edgy. I liked Ring, and I trusted Ring, but only so far. As far as Carboneau and Toby, why, they would stay right here as before, and maybe some day Carboneau would find his treasure. I hoped so! Lord knows he had looked for it long enough. I would miss Toby, though.

I had grown right used to her companionship over the last ten days. She was a fine young woman and were I not so footloose and fancy free, I'd think twice about leaving her. But that was nothing I should be thinking about right now. She'd never leave her grandfather, and he'd never abandon the lost chest of Lafitte. That was his dream, and once a man lost his dream, there wasn't much left to live for. Little did I know that within the next few minutes, all of our dreams would be blown to smithereens.

The shot came unexpectedly, shattering the peace of the

night with an ominous roar. We all jumped, jolted from our own personal moments of reverie. Just a single shot. That was it. Nothing more. The night returned to its peaceful moonlit state without a whimper or a whisper. But not I, nor Toby. We both sensed that something calamitous had happened. Only one of us was missing from our little refuge, and that was Henry Carboneau.

Sometimes he slipped away at night. I had noticed more than once. But he was free to come and go as he wished. We were his guests, and he had no reason to answer to anyone but himself. What he did on his nightly sojourns was his own business, and I had never mentioned his comings and goings.

Toby came up to me silently, the anxiety and fright etched clearly on her face.

'What is it, Dot? What has happened?'

I wanted to reassure her and tell her everything was all right, but it was not in me to coddle or give false hope. We both knew that the shot we had heard was not fired by her grandfather's rifle; we had both heard it fired too many times. This shot was from a big caliber rifle, a Springfield 45.70 or a Winchester 44.40, and the sound was distinctly different. One you would notice immediately, and we both had.

It was too late to be hunting. All game would have bedded long ago and all fowl would have roosted. That shot had not been fired by a hunter. It had been fired by a killer, and whoever he was, he was close by.

'I don't know, Toby,' I responded at last. 'Something's wrong. Your grandfather is out in the woods. He's the only one unaccounted for. He could be hurt, Toby, there's no other way to say it.'

Her hand slipped into mine and she squeezed harder than I thought her capable of.

'If he's hurt I need to go to him. He may not be strong

149

enough to get back on his own.' Her tiny face looked up at me. 'Oh, Dot, please! Don't leave him out there alone!'

She took my other hand in hers, an imploring look on her face. Her grandfather was all she had, almost all she had ever known. The anguish on her face was touching.

'Don't worry. I'll do all I can.' I slipped my right hand from hers and stroked her cheek. She turned her face toward my hand forlornly, seeking any bit of reassurance she could get.

'Your grandpa's a tough old coot. I'll find him and bring him back. You can work your magic on him then.'

Her arms slipped around my neck and she hugged me fiercely, standing on tiptoe as I leaned down to meet her. The scent of her hair was fresh and sweet, as if she used some type of plant or flower to complement her natural smell. I inhaled deeply and when she noticed, she embraced me closer. I held her so for a moment, reluctant to let her go, wanting the moment to last forever. I moved my face from the trusses of her hair and my lips found and gently kissed her neck, then her cheek. I found myself amazed at my forwardness, but somehow it had seemed natural, as if this moment had been predestined long ago.

I released her gently, as a solitary tear slipped from one eye, coursing a damp trail down her silky cheek.

'Be careful, Dot. I couldn't stand it if anything happened to either of you. Find my grandpa and bring him back. I need him!' She wept softly, and as I turned to go, she half sobbed, 'And you too!'

Gathering my rifle, I stopped in the door of the shack. Ring and Antoinette had remained inside and as I appeared, they looked at me expectantly.

'Arm yourself,' I said to Ring, 'I'm going looking for the old man. Keep an eye on her,' I ordered, motioning toward Antoinette with my rifle, 'and watch your back. I'll be back as soon as I can.'

Toby had made me a pair of moccasins and I had taken to wearing them lately. They helped me tonight as I moved through the woods, allowing me to move silently over the leaves and twigs that covered the ground everywhere.

The shot had sounded from the direction of the magnolia grove where we had first rested when bringing the horses to the islet. I knew Carboneau liked to rest there, using the grove as a stopping-over place. He even had a favourite tree that he liked to sit under, and once I had seen him asleep there.

If someone was searching for us, the grove would have offered a likely place to consider. It was the largest area of dry land around, even larger than the islet where we were. Perhaps Carboneau had been surprised there, but I hoped not, for if he had he was more than likely dead.

The night was silent as I made my way cautiously over the land. Carboneau had taught me well, and I covered ground quickly yet silently. I stopped often, my eyes searching every nook and cranny, first for a gunman and secondly for a wounded man.

The moon in the sky provided the only light and as it was a cloudy night, there were times when I could see nothing. Around these intervals, I advanced steadily, listening intently for any sign of another human being.

It took me nearly two hours to close upon the grove, but at last I arrived, and I had done so without the chance of anyone sighting me.

Not a sound broke the silence, yet I waited still. Then, just as I was about to proceed again, I heard a soft moan, low and barely audible. The kind of moan an unconscious man would make. I searched and searched with my eyes, but could see nothing. A cloud passed between the moon and for five minutes I couldn't see the nose on my own face.

The moon came again and this time I heard a scuffing sound, like someone moving an arm or dragging a foot. The sound came from my right, about fifty feet away. The trunk of a huge magnolia rose from the ground and next to it was a vague shadow. A moment passed and the shadow moved, just barely, but enough to allow me to discern the outline of a body.

The moon came again, this time weaker, but I remained in hiding. Whoever had shot Carboneau could still be around waiting to see if anyone came to his aid.

Just as this thought hit me, I caught a glimpse of movement from the corner of my eye, yet above eye level. Swinging my gaze around and upward, I caught the movement again. A boot was descending from a tree and there was a foot in it. A leg followed, and then I could clearly see a man backing down out of the tree. He moved silently, only one small branch making a cracking sound.

When he was safely on the ground, he crouched beneath the tree, his rifle pointed in front of him. He peered in the direction of Carboneau, then quickly around the grove.

I moved not an inch, doing nothing to give my presence away. I had gained the advantage by arriving silently; I would not give it up now.

He rose then, the stalker did, and moved toward Carboneau menacingly. His intent was clear, for even as I watched, he slipped a knife from his belt.

Raising my rifle gently, I waited for a shot. There would be no warning here. He had given none to Carboneau and I would treat him no better. This man was dangerous and did I move or miss my chance, he would turn and shoot me dead.

At every step a tree or limb seemed to forbid a clean shot. He approached the figure on the ground steadily, his knife out and ready.

Gauging his direction against a straight line to Carboneau, I saw that he would have to pass into a clear spot just before he reached the prone figure. That would be my best chance and I would only get one. If I missed, he could disappear behind any of the numerous trees and I would play hell getting Carboneau out then.

He came on and I sighted ahead of him, waiting for his path to cross into the opening. I took up slack in the trigger as he neared, and breathed slowly. On he came, but then at the last possible moment he paused, his body almost entirely behind the last tree before the one under which rested the body of Carboneau.

I eased my finger on the trigger and breathed evenly. The man moved sideways, resting his rifle against the tree that hid his body. His knife gleamed then from the light of the moon as he stepped forward, his knife bent as he intended to kneel next to Carboneau, evidently aiming to finish off his victim at close quarters.

His knee never hit the ground as my shot took him in the side of the head, right near the temple, and his body crashed violently to the side, the knife falling harmlessly from his dead fingers.

Immediately I was up, my pistol now in my right hand as I ran to the stalker. He was dead, killed instantly from my shot. Rolling him over, I saw that it was Corbin White, one of the two most deadly gunmen in Caxton's employ. He had killed many men, but he would kill no more; not unless they fought gun battles in hell.

Carboneau was still alive, but he had lost a lot of blood. He was weak and I needed to get him to help as quickly as possible. If he didn't receive attention soon, he would die.

I gathered up the rifle that lay in the grove. Carboneau's was by his side, Corbin White's propped against the tree. I leaned ours against the tree as well. I couldn't carry

Carboneau and the rifles, so I would have to return for them tomorrow.

As I bent to lift Carboneau, a sound came from behind me. It was a slight sound, but I knew it for what it was. Someone had stepped on a twig and it had cracked under the person's weight.

So I was not alone in the grove. Someone else was here as well. Drawing my pistol, I hid behind the tree under which lay Carboneau. I peered in the direction of the sound, but could see nothing. A minute passed and then another. It was then that I heard the whisper, soft and tentative.

'Dot?'

I started to answer, but fearing a trick, I waited. Again came the query, and I knew without doubt that it was Toby.

'Over here,' I called, stepping from behind the tree so Toby could see me.

She came running, but before she could leap into my arms, she saw her grandfather's figure on the ground. She came to a sliding stop then knelt by his side.

'Is he alive, Dot?'

'Just barely,' I replied. 'Let's get him up and out of here.'

I bent and lifted him into my arms and began to move away. Toby grabbed my arm.

'No, Dot. This way. I brought the canoe.'

Changing directions, I carried Carboneau to the water's edge, having Toby grab the rifle propped against the tree. When all was loaded in the canoe, Toby guided us home, her use of the pole sure and confident.

Ring met us at the bank, still hobbling on his feet but able to get about. As I carried Carboneau to the shack, he gathered up the rifles and brought up the rear.

As Toby worked on her grandfather, Antoinette gave help, boiling water and tearing bandages from an old shirt. The old man had been hit in the shoulder, the force of the bullet knocking him over, his head hitting the tree under which he had lain. The combination of the two blows had knocked him out. He had a nasty lump on his head and had lost a lot of blood from the shoulder wound, but he would survive. Toby had stopped the bleeding and he was resting quietly.

Briefly I told Ring about the set-to in the grove and he seemed pleased to know that Corbin White was out of the fray. As he pointed out, the odds were getting better. Only Caxton, Sawyer Bates, Hondo Cain and Benji Gill remained. Four to one, as I still couldn't count Ring – he was too hobbled.

I stepped outside to think and breathe some fresh air. I wondered if Corbin White had moved on his own or if he had been an advance scout sent by Caxton. If the latter were true, they could be closing on us even now. Those shots could be heard a long ways off and their meaning would be clear to anyone who heard them.

As I stood by the edge of the water, someone came up behind me and I turned, expecting to see Toby. To my surprise, it was Antoinette. She moved close to me, speaking softly in the night.

'Dot, I want to apologize for all the trouble I've caused you. I know you don't believe me and I know you won't trust me, but I'm truly sorry for all I've done.'

When I didn't respond, she shifted her feet nervously and continued.

'Dot, I had no choice but to steal the gold from you. André was pressuring me to marry him, and I had to get away.' She wrung her hands as if for emphasis, but I wasn't buying. 'Then I got the message from Frank, and what could I do? Do you think they would hesitate to kill me? They are not my blood family. Frank was only my stepfather and I'm glad you killed him. He was always mean to me and even more so to my mother.'

As if a sudden idea struck her, she grabbed my hand and said conspiratorially, 'Frank is dead now, Dot. André is recovering at his plantation. Do you know what that means?'

I shook my head and tugged my hand from hers, remembering the last time I had talked to her like this; the night she had shot me in the clearing.

'Don't be like that, Dot! I'm free now. I can do anything I want. Go anywhere I want. Be with anyone I want.' She grabbed my hand again, desperation in her voice. 'We can leave this place, Dot! Just you and I. We can go to San Francisco, or even to St Louis. I'll be yours, Dot, and only yours. You'll see! I'll treat you better than anyone ever could.'

I must admit she was beautiful. The most beautiful woman I had ever known, but her beauty was only skin deep, as the saying went, and I could see through her charade in spite of the effort she put into being earnest. At the first chance, she would kill me like a black widow kills its mate.

'And what about the gold, Antoinette?' I asked gravely. 'What about the gold that belongs to the ranchers in Texas?'

She looked at me as if I'd suddenly grown horns, the disbelief unmistakable in her eyes.

'Why, we take it, Dot! What do you mean? You've earned it! No one else would go this far to protect it. It's yours by right.'

'No, Antoinette, that's where you're wrong. Those ranchers are the only ones who have a right to this gold. They worked for years to raise that herd. Day after day, year after year, they herded those beeves and tended to their every need. They sacrificed everything for those steers, and invested all they had in their safekeeping. Some of them died for that herd, more than one. And how you and your step-family can find it within yourselves to kill and steal it away is beyond me.'

Antoinette released my hand and stepped back a step or two, looking as if she'd been slapped.

'You're a damn fool!' she said hotly. 'You would give all this up for a bunch of stupid ranchers? Look at me!' She smoothed her rumpled dress, arching her breasts at me as if for my perusal. 'Where will you ever find a woman like me? Men would die for me. Men have killed for me. Are you blind?'

'No, I'm not blind, Antoinette, and I've never gainsaid your beauty. There's no question of that. It's your black heart that's ugly, and it's as ugly as I've ever seen.'

She raised her hand as if to strike me, but at my look she thought better of it. Instead, she stated venomously, 'You're a stupid little cowboy, Dot Pickett. You'll never get out of here alive. Caxton will kill you. You can't beat a man like him. He'll see you in hell before you get away with the gold.'

'Be that as it may, Antoinette, you'll never see a penny of it. Now get back inside before I gag you and tie you again.'

She wanted to say more, to strike me, to hurt me, to kill me – anything – but she was powerless to do so and she knew it. Her only recourse lay in Caxton. He was coming and she knew it as well as I.

With a huff she swirled around and left me alone at the water's edge. I was glad she was gone, for fighting with her would accomplish nothing. The real fight was coming, and it was coming soon.

CHAPTER FIFTEEN

Toby gave me a funny look as I entered the shack. She was sitting next to her grandfather, who was resting easily, his breathing shallow but regular.

Ring was busy cleaning the rifle that had belonged to Corbin White and Antoinette had angrily retired beneath her blanket, her back to us. But she was not asleep. More than likely she was planning some new method of creating mayhem and disruption, if not outright murder.

It would be daylight in a few hours. I had hoped that we could pull out then and take our chances with breaking through any line of sentinels Caxton may have deployed, but Carboneau's wounding had ruled out that possibility. I could still pull out on my own, taking Ring with me, but I could not abandon the old man and Toby now. They wouldn't even be in this predicament had I never intruded into their world. We were all in this together now, for better or worse. Worrying at it would do me no good. I was tired and morning was just around the corner. If I didn't get some sleep soon, I'd be no good to anybody.

The smell of coffee and frying bacon woke me and it was a pleasant way to greet the morning. Only Toby was up and she stood smiling next to an old potbellied stove, a spatula in her hand and a stray wisp of hair cross her face. She poured me a cup of coffee and I accepted it gratefully.

A moment later Ring was up, and together we broke fast. There was little conversation, each of us content to enjoy the peace of the morning silently. Antoinette slept on from her place in the corner, and we left her be.

After we had eaten, Toby fed her grandfather some broth she had made and then a little soup. He looked much better already, the colour having returned to his face. He had suffered only a flesh wound and although it had bled profusely, he would recover quickly.

I left the shack then, giving Ring orders to stay close and to keep a close watch on Antoinette. I wanted to scout about and cut for sign. Those shots last night could have been heard by anyone and I didn't want to be caught off guard.

I made for the magnolia grove where I had killed Corbin White last night. I had left his body when it had fallen and it was my intent to dispose of it this morning. If our shots had been heard and men came looking, there was nothing like a dead man to let them know we were close at hand.

My moccasins were stiff this morning from all the wading I had done last night. By the time I made the grove they were soaked again, but had limbered up.

There appeared to be no one around, but I approached cautiously nonetheless. Appearances had cost more than a few men their lives, and I was in no hurry to join them.

When I came to the tree under which Carboneau had lain and where Corbin White had fallen when I shot him, there was no body. At first I thought I had the wrong tree, but a closer scrutiny only verified that this was the tree. Naturally, I took cover, not knowing if Caxton or his men had discovered the body and moved it and were therefore still close by. But after a half hour had passed, I was sure that I was the only one in the grove.

I examined the ground beneath the tree closely and eventually found where Carboneau had bled into the ground. Next I found the same evidence of Corbin White, but the body was gone. The tracks that Toby and I had made were still evident upon the ground, but there were no other human tracks since.

It was then that I noticed what appeared to be some type of claw marks, as if some beast had landed and flew off with the body. A shudder swept over me then and involuntarily I glanced about me quickly.

As I examined the marks closer, a vague trail became discernible in the soft ground. The leaves and twigs upon the ground had been displaced and once I noticed that, the trail was easy to follow, as something had dragged Corbin White's body away. What creature was big enough to do that? I wondered.

My first thought was that a lion of some type had carried the body away, but there were no mountain lions around here that I had ever heard of and although there were wildcats and bobcats, they were much too small to drag off a man.

A little further on, I came upon a pistol. It must have fallen from Corbin White's holster as the beast dragged him along. I had overlooked it last night, but I scooped it up now and tucked it beneath my gun belt.

The trail became clearer as I neared the water and a path of sorts became apparent. Soon I faced a slough, and the trail disappeared within its murky depths. Void of leaves here, the trail was of mud and it was a wide, slick trail. The claw marks were clear then, as well as the sweeping marks made by a large tail. It was a 'gator that had found Corbin White's body. Whether by smell or happenstance, I didn't know, but it had sure enough dragged him off into the water. For the second time this morning a shudder swept over me. Nature worked quick in the bayous.

I searched the entire grove and found no sign of anyone other than those of us who had been here the night before. I had wondered at how Corbin White had found this grove and how he had reached this destination. I found no sign of horse or boat and I remembered distinctly that Corbin White had been wearing boots last night. He couldn't have waded in, as his boots would have prohibited his even trying to do so, but he couldn't have flown, either.

I redoubled my efforts at discovering a boat of some type, perhaps a canoe or flatboat like Carboneau had hidden about. But there was no sign of anything.

Having made almost a complete semi-circular search of the northern tip of the grove, I had about decided that it didn't matter when I heard the voices. Two of them, and they were speaking in French.

Taking cover quickly, I listened as they approached. I could understand nothing they were saying, but they were coming closer – of that there was no doubt.

Then another voice spoke and I recognized it instantly. At that very moment, they came into sight. It was Caxton Banks, in a flatboat, with two Cajun guides. His gunmen were with him, also; all of them, or at least all that remained. Sawyer Bates, Hondo Cain and Benji Gill; and they were loaded for bear. I had never seen so many guns. Rifles pointed everywhere and pistols and knives were abundantly displayed. If guns were quills, they would look like a boat full of porcupines.

The two Cajuns guided the boat to shore, the younger of the two stepping out and heaving the nose higher on to the bank.

They debarked hurriedly, Caxton giving orders to the Cajuns, who quickly began to build a fire. The rest spread out around the fire, producing cups from their gear.

161

Caxton Banks peered south into the grove, apparently looking for someone, and it was then that I realized he was looking for Corbin White. They must have dropped him off here last night to scout about and were now returning to pick him up. Perhaps the others had already been picked up from other locations with the same purpose.

'This is the place, isn't it?' Caxton's voice came clearly to me as he inquired in English of the Cajuns. They only nodded and returned to their coffee. 'Then where the hell is he?'

Sawyer Bates rose to his feet, cupping his own cup of coffee in two big hands. 'He's around somewhere, boss. Probably asleep. He never was one for early rising.'

Sawyer Bates whistled then, a sharp, piercing whistle, using two fingers at his mouth. When he received no response, he whistled again. A moment later he shrugged his shoulders and squatted near the fire, sipping his coffee slowly.

Caxton Banks, turning to the younger of the two Cajuns, said, 'Cast about and find Corbin. Tell him to get over here pronto.'

The Cajun rose and headed south. It wouldn't take him long to discover that Corbin White was not in the grove. If he was half as good as the other Cajuns in these parts, it wouldn't take him long to find the blood on the ground and he'd read that story like you and I would read the pages of a book. Once that cat was out of the bag, I'd best be long gone, as my tracks were like a signature all over this grove.

I should have taken more care in covering my sign, and I should have eliminated all evidence of the blood under the big magnolia, and the trail leading from it to the slough where the 'gator had fled with Corbin White's body. But I had not expected Caxton and his crew to suddenly appear in a boat, so I had allowed my guard to slip. Well, what's done was done and there was nothing I could do about it now. The only thing left for me to do was beat a hasty retreat before I was the next one feeding the 'gators.

I began a cautious retreat, taking care to move as silently as possible as I edged away from their camp. The older Cajun by the fire was paying no attention to the camp and the idle conversation around it. Instead, he seemed to be focused on the woods surrounding the camp. He didn't search the grove with his eyes, as they stared blankly at the coffee in his cup. But it seemed eerily obvious to me that he was searching every inch of the grove with his ears. His attentiveness made me doubly wary, as within this man I sensed an uncommon foe.

Once I was about a hundred yards from the camp, I began to move more swiftly, putting distance between myself and the wood-wise Cajun.

His partner would be somewhere ahead of me, and between myself and a direct path to the bayou shack where Toby and the gold awaited my return. I would have to take care to skirt wide around the southern tip of the grove to avoid contact with him as he searched futilely for Corbin White. This would be difficult as the southern tip narrowed noticeably as it sank beneath the water level. From that point on, the water was knee to waist deep all the way to the tiny islet that was our refuge. I had waded this distance without mishap before, more than once, but now I found myself compelled to take a different line.

In so keeping, I moved to the very southeast edge of the grove and here it became a tangle of low growing vines, brush and shrubs. I waded into the water in an effort to pass silently, but a sudden drop off in the bottom caused me to retrace my path.

The water was murky here and almost stagnant, and deeper than what I had traversed before. At every step, I was careful to hold my rifle above water level lest a sudden drop off submerged my weapons as well as myself. My gun belt I had removed and now wore looped around my neck, the extra pistol of Corbin White's tied to an empty bullet loop with a piggin string I always carried in my pocket.

By the time I had cleared the tangle that had prevented me from returning in a direct line to the shack, I was considerably off course. But safe, I believed, from detection. I must get safely back to the shack and warn everyone of Caxton's presence. To be caught before then would mean an almost certain death.

The bottom began to rise now and soon I was only ankle deep in water, and in some places I passed over level ground. I was still about a half a mile from the islet and must take a cattycornered line to return. I should now have been safely below the young Cajun, who by now would have discovered the spot where Corbin White had died. If he returned directly to their camp with the news, and they immediately loaded into the flatboat to come around the grove, they would still be a half hour behind me. Granted, they could move faster in the boat than I could on foot, but I should still be safe as long as I kept moving.

Nevertheless, there was something about the older Cajun at the camp that made me leery. He had a look, a presence even, about him that bespoke an inordinately dangerous and savvy man. He reminded me of some of the Comanche warriors I had seen and dealt with in Texas, and anyone who knew beans about Indians knew that the Comanche was among the most dangerous of warring Indians.

Bearing this in mind, I proceeded prudently, yet even my heightened vigilance didn't prepare me for what happened next.

Passing around a huge clump of cypress trees whose

branches, limbs and exposed roots blocked my view momentarily, I spied Caxton's boat full of gunmen and Cajun guides coming straight at me. We saw each other at the same instant, but my response was quicker. I palmed my pistol and shot the young Cajun who was at the prow of the boat. He tumbled silently into the shallow water as the rest of the boat's occupants dove for cover.

There was plenty of cover all around, as live oaks and cypress trees were everywhere. It was difficult to move in a straight line in any direction as the trees always dictated one's course. Any path I chose was a snaky one, subject to the whims of nature. It was this distinction that saved me from being killed out of hand as I disappeared behind the clump of cypress trees and beat a hasty retreat.

The density of the trees that had first caused the confrontation now saved my life, as I used their cover to separate from Caxton and his men. A sporadic shot or two came from behind me, but it was only a searching fire and had small chance of hitting anything other than bark.

My retreat was far from silent, yet I paid little attention to the noise I made. My first concern was to put as much distance between myself and Caxton's men as possible. Once, I paused and thought I heard a similar noise to that of my own from my left, but it didn't sound again and I continued on.

The only good thing about my retreat was that it was taking Caxton and his men further away from our refuge. But the converse was that I myself was ranging farther from safety.

There was no doubt that those at the shack would hear these shots and be forewarned. But there was little hope of help for me. Ring was still too feeble to be of any good to me out here, and it would be a few days yet before Carboneau was ambulatory.

165

A slight rise appeared before me and I gratefully took to the dry ground. Moving to the highest point on this plot of acreage, I came upon a live oak taller than most I had seen. Quickly lifting myself up by the lowest limbs, I clambered up among the protecting foliage and observed my backtrail.

At first I saw nothing. Then in the distance, about a thousand yards away, I spied the flatboat that had emptied so ardently a few moments earlier. It was reoccupied and moving cautiously toward me. Benji was now at the prow, with Caxton, Sawyer Bates and Hondo Cain behind him. The latter two were rowing steadfastly, taking their cue and instruction from Benji Gill, who was acting point as they moved resolutely forward.

The Cajun was absent and I roved left and right, my eyes trying to pick him up. I swept farther out with my gaze, but still failed to find him. Slowly, I began a more methodical search, observing every bit of cover between the flatboat and myself, but after a few moments I had still failed to pick him up. Perhaps he had stayed behind with the other Cajun, giving assistance to the man. Yet, by the way he had toppled from the boat and the surety of my aim, I was sure he was dead.

As I began to search once more for the Cajun, I remembered the sound I had thought I heard to my left in the early moments of my flight; the sound that had ceased almost in harmony with my own movement.

I became uneasy and twisted around in an attempt to inspect a more advanced area to my left and to the northeast from my position in the tree. It was then that the shot sounded and a terrible blow struck me in the side. The force of the blow knocked me loose from my perch in the tree and I tumbled out and down, striking a few thick limbs as I fell. My neck was the first thing that struck the ground and lucky it was that the ground was soft, or I'd have likely broke my fool neck.

Stunned, I nevertheless drew my pistol as I lay full upon the ground, rolling over to peer in the direction from whence had come the shot. My skull was ringing from my fall and a dull ache issued from my side.

I saw the Cajun then, and he was running full out in my direction, intent upon finishing his kill. My body was hidden by the trunk of the live oak and my face was masked by low lying shrubbery and fallen limbs.

The Cajun came on and I snapped a shot at him. It was a clean miss, but it arrested his attack as he dove for cover.

My rifle was by my side, but I preferred the pistol for close work. Although I could not see the Cajun now, I fired a shot in his direction anyway. It would buy me time and as my senses were still befuddled, it would help.

My hand checked the spot where the bullet had struck me on my side. Fortunately, the bullet had hit my gun belt at an angle and although it had destroyed a loop, it had drawn no blood. I would have a bruise, but that was fine, considering the alternative.

Desperately, I searched for sight of the Cajun. Our shots would have drawn the attention of those in the boat and they would be closing fast. To wait for them to draw nigh would ensure my death. I must move now and without hesitation.

I fired another shot in the general direction of where I thought the Cajun to be. It smacked loudly into a tree and I rose to my feet, half running, half stumbling as I strove to put distance between he and I.

A shot sang over my head and another struck a tree to my right, shooting bits of bark and tree splinters into my face.

I continued my rapid retreat, pausing to fire in the direction of the Cajun, never getting a clear shot at him and fortunate that he was unable to hit me as I zigzagged behind trees and whatever other cover I could find.

On one blind shot behind me, I heard a yip and I hoped I had scored a lucky hit. But the Cajun's pursuit never wavered, and we continued on until the rise of dry land ended abruptly in dark, lethargic water. I plunged in, heedful of not just the Cajun behind, but of those in the boat who I could even now hear clomping overland as they rushed to aid the Cajun.

Caxton and his men in the boat pursued me at a right angle and their direction had allowed them to close quickly. My only fire had been directed at the Cajun, so Caxton and his men had come on without fear of punition. I could see them now as they scurried through the trees to my right, an occasional shot fired hastily in my direction. Their course forced me to swing to my left as they would intercept me soon.

Still the Cajun closed, and this time one of his shots found its mark. A searing pain erupted from my left shoulder as his bullet struck me from behind. I blundered forward, almost losing my balance, striking a tree with my right shoulder as another bullet struck near me, this one from Caxton's men who closed on my right.

I fell then, going to my knees in the dank water. I was fairly trapped and would have to make a last stand right here. There would be no rescue for me as my friends were far away, and Caxton's men were converging on me from the right, the perilous Cajun on my left.

Rising shakily to my feet, I took cover behind a cypress whose trunk had been split by a lightning strike, causing it to grow in a fork. I lay my rifle in the crotch of the fork and took aim.

From what was my left now as I turned to face my pursuers, Caxton's men came blindly on. My best chance for a hit was Benji Gill, who appeared not a hundred feet away. I took up slack in the trigger and squeezed her off. He let out a scream of agony as the bullet took him in the groin, and all pursuit ceased. Each man took cover behind whatever best afforded them protection.

Benji Gill lay plainly in sight as he writhed in agony and I could have killed him then and there, but I preferred to leave him be, as his screams would demoralize the others and put a damper on their inclinations to close with me.

I sought another target, but everyone seemed to be content to remain behind cover, probably catching their breath – like me – and keeping their heads down to avoid a similar fate as that of Benji Gill.

His misery was still clearly audible as he now called for someone to come to his aid. No one answered and no one moved, and Benji's calls began to diminish as his body went into shock.

Sporadic fire began to search me, and twice I clearly heard Caxton calling to his men, positioning them as they fanned out in front of me.

Behind me not ten feet away, a small stream swept by and had I not stopped where I had, I would have stumbled into its depths. It didn't appear to be deep, not more than four or five feet, but even so, it would have submerged me and all my weapons would have been soaked, if not swept from my hands by the surprisingly swift current.

The benefit was that it would check the advance of Caxton and his men and disallow any attempt to get behind me, at least for the moment. The odds were dwindling fast and only Caxton Banks, Sawyer Bates and Hondo Cain remained of the original group. Those three would stay together, as they were gunmen, not woodsmen, and the only one wily enough to consider – let alone attempt – to get behind me would be the Cajun.

The afternoon wore on and soon evening approached. I knew those at the islet would be wondering what had happened, their senses alert for any sound or shot. Ring could not move well enough yet to round up the horses, load the gold in the canoe and lead them out to dry land. He was a Cajun, true, and bayou smart. But the way in to the islet had been difficult and tricky and Carboneau had led the way.

Ring had been delirious with pain and half out of his senses. He had ridden in the flatboat, oblivious to all that went on around him, and wouldn't remember heads or tails of the trip that had brought us to the tiny inland islet.

Even so, I worried for Toby if I didn't return, with her grandfather down and out for the time being.

My shoulder was beginning to pain me fearfully, and I gathered fallen Spanish moss and, together with mud, I made a compress to pack against the wound. The coolness of the mud helped and I applied another compress to the front where the bullet had exited. I was lucky in that the bullet had passed cleanly through the upper part of my shoulder, missing bone and exiting without causing great damage. It had bled a lot, but my quick application of the compress had staunched the flow and the pain began to ebb as I watched for any sign of my pursuers.

It had been a while since a shot had been fired and, throughout the duration of my stand, I had heard nothing from the Cajun. This caused me great agitation as he was the most capable and deadly of the men aligned against me. No news from him was bad news, as he was more than probably up to something. He was the one to watch, as he had slipped up on me once already.

My reminiscence was interrupted by a call from Caxton.

'Dot! Dot Pickett! This is Caxton Banks. Give us the gold and we'll let you go.'

I ignored him, knowing that there could be no negotiating with him and that to enter into a debate would only be a waste of time and energy.

At my silence, he continued.

'You're trapped, Dot. There's no getting away this time. Just give us the gold. Tell us where it is and we'll let you go. Hell, you can even keep some of it. There's enough for everyone. You've seen to that. You've killed half my men already. It'll be a bigger split for everyone.'

I wasn't splitting anything with anyone and he knew it. He was only trying to draw a response from me, perhaps hoping that I would show myself and allow his men a shot at me.

Until now, all my shots had originated from the crotch of the fork in the old cypress. My rifle rested there now as I kept my head behind the trunk. Slipping my rifle from its rest, I lay prone on the ground, peeking around the trunk at ground level. Sliding my rifle ahead of me, I gazed in the direction of Caxton's voice. I had spotted the tree that he was behind earlier, and I looked for him there now.

Sure enough, a moment later as he called to me I saw the brim of his hat poke from around his tree.

'Come on, Dot. Let's end this here without anyone else getting hurt.'

I noticed as he spoke that he leaned forward slightly, causing part of his face to come into view.

I aimed carefully, taking up slack in the trigger. I didn't have to wait long, as a moment later he called again. He only got one word out – my name – as I fired as soon as his nose came into view.

He screamed wildly as he sprang away from the tree, his entire body coming into view on the other side of the tree as he slapped wildly at his face. Even from my position, I could see the blood that appeared suddenly on his hands.

Allowing him no reprieve, I fired twice more in quick succession. One struck the tree, the other his boot, knocking his leg out from under him. Somehow he ended up back

171

behind his tree and I held my fire, his shrieks and cursing ringing loudly over the evening dusk.

'You shot my nose off, you son of a bitch! You're a dead man, Pickett! A dead man!'

More muffled wails of agony came from behind Caxton's tree and I broke my silence.

'You asked for it, by God. Now shut the hell up and take it like a man!'

Caxton bellowed something incoherently, then called to Sawyer Bates and Hondo Cain.

'Get him, damn it! Blow his damn head off!'

The woods erupted in a hail of gunfire, my poor old cypress tree taking a beating. I hunkered safely behind my wooden fortification until at last the gunfire waned. I could still hear Caxton's cursing and I hadn't heard anyone curse like that since I rode a piece once with a mule train. Those mule skinners could sure enough curse, but Caxton was right up there with them.

I returned my rifle to the crotch in the tree, keeping my head down, yet alert for any advance by Caxton and his men. None came and darkness would soon be upon us. I would have to make my move then to get out of here, as I was fairly trapped as it was.

It was then that the ground not ten feet from me spewed forth an angry Cajun, a knife in his hand and hatred in his eyes. How he had managed to get so close to me I couldn't explain, but he was there and death came with him.

I turned to meet his charge but was unable to bring my rifle to bear. I clutched my rifle helplessly as he swung his knife overhanded and plunged the blade toward my chest. It struck solidly, the tip of the blade sinking deeply into the stock of my rifle which I held protectively across my chest, seeking to ward off his attack. We struggled, then as he refused to let go of the knife, there was a tug-of-war between two desperate men, each trying earnestly to kill the other.

The Cajun wrenched mightily against his knife and it came free, a chunk of wood from the stock still stuck to the tip. He tried to stab me again and this time he got through my defenses, his thrust taking me full in the breast. But the chunk of wood from the stock of my rifle prevented penetration and his thrust proved futile.

We grappled again then, stumbling dangerously from the protection of the old cypress. Caxton and his men held their fire, afraid of hitting the Cajun. But then a shot rang out heedlessly, buzzing over our heads like an angry bee.

We were face to face, the Cajun and I, our struggle taking us even further from the tree. He slashed at me with the edge of his knife, trying to slice my throat and spill my life's blood upon the ground, and I leaned back from his strike, the blade missing me by inches.

Another shot rang out, closely followed by a second and then a third. The Cajun tugged vigorously at the rifle and purposely I let go with my right hand, the sudden loss of resistance causing his body to swing to my left, and quickly I palmed my pistol and shot him in the chest. My foot came out from under me then and I fell sideways. The Cajun steadfastly clung to the rifle, my fall dragging us both to the ground where we rolled once and fell into the stream.

We were both immediately submerged and when I returned to the surface, my hand was the only one left clutching at the rifle. The current was surprisingly rapid, and I felt the Cajun's body bump past me, his hand surfacing as he rolled in the current, then disappearing again beneath the swirling eddy.

Gasping for air as the current dragged me with it, I saw Caxton, Sawyer Bates and Hondo Cain at the water's edge, their pistols levelled at me as I was swept away by the current. Startled, I sank below the surface as their bullets sought me, at least two striking me, their path through the water slowing their velocity enough to prevent a wounding.

I held my breath for as long as I could, relaxing my body and allowing the current to whisk me away. When I again resurfaced, Caxton and his men were nowhere to be seen. I was sure they would follow me, so I kicked out with my feet and began to swim with the current, deliberately crossing to the far side of the stream.

It was dark now and the distance I had covered was enough to provide me safety. Their chase would have to end, as the darkness and the density of the trees would allow little room for a rapid pursuit. Once the moon had risen, a man could see well enough to move about, but until then I would be safe.

Crawling out on the far side of the stream, I slipped up the bank and on to dry land. I still clutched my rifle in my left hand and my pistol in my right. I would need to clean them and dry them as soon as possible, and I sought shelter by which to do so. The night was still early and before the sun rose in the morning, the moon would shine its pallid light on a bloody ground.

CHAPTER SIXTEEN

It was a cold camp I made, if a camp it could even be called. I stripped from my clothes, hanging them in various limbs about me. I had nothing with which to make a fire, so any hope of my clothes drying completely was in vain.

I cleaned my weapons as best I could and dried them thoroughly with Spanish moss and the breath from my very lungs. I regarded the breach in the stock of my rifle in wonderment, awed by the whimsical nature of fate. How such a quirk had saved my life was humbling, and I gave silent thanks to the gods, whoever they may be.

After an hour had passed, I dressed and gathered my weapons. Following the stream in a southerly direction, I looked for a place to cross. It didn't take long to find one as I came upon a shallow about a mile downstream. I crossed quickly and cut inland and diagonally from the stream in a direction that would bring me back on course for our sanctuary. This would be a dangerous path to take as the possibility of crossing with Caxton and his men was high, but I was armed and I would be ready.

In my struggle with the Cajun, the compress of mud and Spanish moss that I had made for my shoulder wound had come loose and fallen away, but I had made another at my cold camp, tearing loose a piece of my shirt to tie it securely to the wound. I had used the better part of the bottom of my shirt, which now hung in tatters around my waist, but I felt better and I moved with a confidence that gave me courage.

Urgently I moved across the marshland, disrupting the calls of bullfrogs, crickets and katydids. Owls hooted from their perches in the highest limbs, but quieted at my passing. Once I disrupted the roosting of a flock of turkeys, whose heavy beating flapping to flight left a wake of feathers floating gently to the ground.

I crossed dry ground and wet ground, high and low, my course taking me almost parallel to the route I had taken during my flight from Caxton and the Cajun. By the time the sun was beginning to rise, I was only about a quarter of a mile from where I fought with the Cajun and had fallen into the stream, at last heading back to our tiny islet, which had been my original destination.

I had seen no sign of Caxton and his men, the two that he had left to him. But I knew they were somewhere close. They would be lurking about, determined, even if discouraged, to end this once and for all. Caxton would be ill tempered, to say the least, with most of his nose shot off, but that was no concern of mine. You reap what you sow, as the saying goes, and Caxton had been sowing bad seed for quite some time.

It was then that I saw the body. I was crossing a small clearing, wary of an ambush, when I caught a patch of color out of the corner of my eye. I stopped and took a position behind a tree, scouting for the presence of others as I peered in the direction of the patch of blue that had caught my attention. Advancing cautiously, I soon discovered that the blue was that of Benji Gill's jeans, and he was propped against a tree, his eyes dull and unseeing. He had been abandoned by his comrades, and he had been dead quite some time.

They had divested him of his weapons, leaving him to die

in solitude, but there was nothing I could do for him, as I had nothing with which to bury him even if the ground would hold his body.

I moved on, leaving Benji Gill to the forces of nature. I had travelled about a mile and was making good time when I smelled smoke. Few things could be a truer indication of man's presence than smoke, and I pulled up expectantly.

It was Caxton, Sawyer Banks and Hondo Cain; the last remaining three. They sat dejectedly around a miserable fire that was more smoke than flame, Caxton holding his face in his hands, his arms and shirtfront covered in dried blood.

Sawyer Bates and Hondo Cain stared solemnly into the fire. Their appearance was bedraggled at best, and a more woebegone look I had never seen. Their clothes were dishevelled and they were wet from head to toe. Hondo Cain had a boot missing, steam rising from his socked foot that he extended toward the fire. His shirt was open to the neck, the undershirt beneath soiled and stained with blood. He had a wound to his neck, but it was only slight and he would live. At least for a while longer.

Sawyer Bates had his pistol in his lap as he went through the motions of cleaning it. A rifle leaned against his leg, and I noted that to arm himself he would have to drop the pistol and reach for the rifle.

The three of them were totally oblivious to my presence, and even as I stepped into their camp, they failed to detect my appearance for a long moment. It was Caxton who seemed to sense something and he looked up gloomily.

'You son of a bitch!' he spat at me. 'You've played hob. How dare you walk into my camp and look at me like that.'

Sawyer Bates and Hondo Cain had froze once they noticed me and they sat unmoving, staring at me dully.

'You've got a gun,' I answered. 'Use it if you don't like it.'

He stared at me coldly, and I could see the damage my

177

bullet had done to his nose. It wasn't completely gone, but the tip was missing and what remained looked like it had been chewed by a mad dog.

The confident, dapper man that I had first known in Abilene was gone. He had been hard and self-assured there, even arrogant in his demeanor, as he had bragged amongst his friends of what he would do to me. But his boastful attitude had been replaced by a sullen, bedraggled, beaten look. The long weeks on the trail and our gun battles here in the bayous had acted as an auger, and the true man had at last been exposed and it was not a pretty picture. He was battered. He was defeated. He was thoroughly bested, but he was still dangerous, like a cornered rat or a trapped coyote, and if ever he could, he would take someone with him.

I pointed my rifle at him, which I carried in my left hand, my right free to draw my pistol if the need arose.

'Stand up, Caxton,' I said callously. 'Drop your pistol on the ground.'

He only ignored me, staring at me hatefully.

'Move it, Caxton. Drop your pistol or be shot.'

'Go to hell,' he said brashly. 'Shoot me!'

He stuck his chin out, as if daring me to do so – and I shot him.

The shot surprised everyone, especially Caxton, whom I assume believed I would banter with him. But to me, the time for talk was over and had been for a long time.

My bullet took him in his left armpit, knocking him over and backwards from the log he sat on.

Sawyer Bates and Hondo Cain were sitting on the bare ground and they both grabbed wildly at their guns. Palming my pistol, I fired twice at Hondo Cain, knowing he would get into action before Sawyer Bates. One shot was a clean miss, the other striking him somewhere in the midsection.

With my left, I fired blindly at Caxton, who was scrambling about on all fours, searching frantically among the foliage for the pistol that had slipped from its holster during his tumble.

Sawyer Bates now had his rifle and as he brought it to bear, I fired my pistol carefully and precisely, the heavy .45 slug taking him squarely in the throat, severing his spine as it exited from the back of his neck. He dropped like a rag doll and lay there, dead and unmoving.

To my left, Caxton had at last made it to his feet, his pistol clutched desperately in his hand. But instead of turning to face me, he began to run, screaming incoherently as he fled among the trees.

Returning my attention to Hondo Cain, he was the only one of the three who got off a shot, and he, only one. It whizzed by harmlessly and I fired twice in rapid succession, both shots taking him fairly in the chest. He stopped his pistol, swaying slightly on his feet before toppling sideways to lay next to Sawyer Bates, companions to the end, even in death, their eyes open but unseeing.

In the distance, I could hear Caxton Banks crashing madly through the woods. Reloading my pistol, I listened to his progress, gauging his direction and judging the route I would take to chase him down.

A more compassionate man might have let him go, knowing that he was beat and wounded, and more likely than not destined to wander aimlessly until he died, either from his wound or from the elements. But I was not a compassionate man. Not to my enemies, leastways. Such sympathies could cause a man to die, and I was in no hurry to do so from neglect.

Once my pistol was reloaded, I gathered the weapons of Sawyer Bates and Hondo Cain and placed them on their inert forms. I would return for them later, being a man not wont to waste.

Caxton Banks had fled in a northerly direction and I followed him slowly. I could not hear him now, but his trail was easy to follow, being defined clearly by the drops of blood that marked his passage.

The woods became thick and tangled as I continued my pursuit. Like a wounded animal, Caxton had chosen the most intractable direction in which to flee, instinctively seeking to throw off his pursuer. Doggedly I followed, knowing that he would have to turn and fight in the end, his condition too far gone to allow him to outdistance me.

Heedful of this, my pursuit slowed as I put caution ahead of speed. This would be when he was most dangerous. Wounded, hurt, frightened, desperate and bayed, he would kill anything he saw, anything that approached him. He had run earlier, but once he could run no longer he would fight tooth and claw, root hog or die, and I was determined not to give him that chance.

The terrain began to slope downward and soon I was wading in ankle deep water. This lasted for about a hundred yards and I lost Caxton's trail momentarily. But as the land rose again, I picked up his trail once more, spying the droplets of blood on the ground, the overturned leaves and twigs only verifying his passage.

From ahead I heard a twig crunch and I knew I was close. Again, the land rose, forming a hummock about forty square feet in area. I approached this with extreme caution, moving from one tree to another.

A shot rang out and a bullet smacked into the tree next to me. Ducking my head, I ran quickly to the next tree, stopping in time to hear a muffled crash ahead, then a barely audible splashing sound.

Cresting the hummock, I saw Caxton high-stepping through shin high water. The trees and ever-present Spanish moss half blocking my view of him, he was fifty yards out when I reached the edge of the water. His back was to me and he was labouring severely, intent only upon putting distance between himself and me.

I was about to call his name when he stumbled and fell, his body half submerging in the shallow water. Lurching to his feet, he took another faltering step, then sank to his waist as the water apparently deepened. His pistol was extended over his head as he vainly tried to keep it dry.

Desperately he called to me.

'Go away, Pickett! Leave me alone!'

I stepped closer to the water's edge, ignoring him as I did. Beneath my feet an old path could barely be seen, as if at some time long ago a trail or road had once passed through here.

'I've had enough,' Caxton yelled once more, tossing his pistol into the water. 'I'm unarmed, Dot. You can't shoot me now. Back off and leave me be. I'll not harm you any more.'

He was making this difficult. Extremely difficult, as although I wanted him dead, it went against my nature to shoot an unarmed man – even one like Caxton.

He was still waist deep in water, his arms now held high in a gesture of surrender. I couldn't shoot him now, and he knew it. His breathing was laboured and his face was pale. He was dying, and he knew it as well as I.

Holstering my pistol, I called out to him.

'All right, Caxton, wade on up here and I'll give you a hand.'

I stepped almost into the water and held my hand out encouragingly. A look of relief passed over his face and he dropped his hands and came forward. I waited as he paused, obviously having great difficulty in moving through the waist deep water.

Then his right leg rose and his knee came out of the

water. He had stepped up on to something – a submerged log or tree stump – and he rose swiftly from the water, the placid look of relief on his face being replaced by one of outright hate and triumph.

Clearing the water with only his boots now submerged, he unerringly reached behind his back and drew another pistol which I had not noticed before. He shifted his feet slightly to take aim at me, our actions as one as I drew my own pistol and fired.

From beneath the water came a dull crunching sound, as of something giving way, and Caxton's left leg plunged back into the water, causing him to topple sideways even as my bullet struck him on the breastbone, his own shot flying harmlessly into the air as his arms flew high over his head.

As his body continued to topple over, his leg broke, the snapping sound drawing a hideous scream from his mouth. His head disappeared beneath the surface and his scream was cut off by the murky water. He twitched a few times, his leg still trapped in something beneath the water. Then at last he lay still, the life finally fleeing from his body.

Reluctantly, I waded out to him, intending to at least free him so his body could slip beneath the surface and find whatever peace it could. The water rose only to my knees or so, then just before I reached him it deepened. Feeling around with my feet, I found an old root system from a long dead tree, the roots were as big around as my thigh and completely undetectable from the water's edge. Caxton was only a few feet from me and whatever he had stepped on to had been entwined in the roots, trapped among their encircling embrace.

Using the roots to bridge the short distance from me to Caxton, I quickly crossed to him. I grabbed his leg and tugged gently, then more forcefully. His foot slipped from his boot and came free and I gently pushed him into his watery grave.

It took me an instant to discover exactly what he had stepped on to. It was not a stump or log, as I had originally imagined. As I felt around beneath the surface, I discovered the hole his foot had caused, and prying loose a piece of wood, I brought it to surface. It was rounded and had obviously been shaped by human hands. It was waterlogged, but nevertheless sturdy. Its colour was dark, with a lighter coloured band running across its surface where evidently a metal band or strip had once rested, or covered its surface, protecting it from the wear and tear that the rest of it had suffered. The wood itself was arched in shape, but the piece I had was too small to allow identification.

Further exploration below the surface brought my fingers into contact with metal, and after a few minutes of tugging and wrenching, I was able to pry it free. It was a hasp of some sort and the band that it had been attached to was rusted and had at last broken free at my ministrations. Cleaning it of mud and encrustations, I could make out letters of some sort evidently stamped into the surface of the metal. When at last I had cleaned it thoroughly, a name was clearly discernible. I read it out loud: *Jean Lafitte*, below which was a date: *1821*.

I took a deep breath in awe and almost fell into the water. This was the lost sea chest of Jean Lafitte, the pirate and brigand that Henry Carboneau had told me about! This was the treasure that he had spent at least fifty years searching for, and I, purely by chance, had discovered it. Or at least, Caxton Banks had.

The enormity of it struck me and I knew I had to go for Carboneau. This had been his dream for most of his adult life, and he deserved to be here.

There was no budging the chest from its watery resting place, so I knew it would be safe until we could return. I would have no trouble finding this place again, but just in case, I used my knife to cut markings in trees as I made my way back to the bayou shack where Toby and my own treasure awaited my return.

CHAPTER SEVENTEEN

The sun was directly overhead when I at last returned to the bayou shack. It was a nervous bunch that greeted me, only Toby and Old Man Carboneau showing signs of relief and joy at my return.

I held my hand up at their inquiries, expressing my desires to eat and rest first. At this, Toby disappeared inside the shack while Ring and Antoinette wandered off together. I watched them as they went, curious as to Ring's true intentions and loyalties.

Old Man Carboneau had been resting on a pallet outside when I returned, his rifle by his side as he had tried to read the story of my fight from the sounds of the shots they had all clearly heard.

I joined him now, sitting next to him with my back propped against the shack.

He allowed me my rest and peace, asking no questions, yet obviously content that I had returned alive, and for the most part, not seriously hurt.

Shortly, Toby returned with a plate full of stew, with at least three kinds of meat in it. I wolfed it down and ate another, devouring eight pieces of cornbread in the process. I chased it all down with hot coffee and, at last sated, placed the plate next to me and sighed.

I slept the rest of the day away and on through the night and into the next morning. No one bothered me and when at last I awoke, I felt as if the world had been lifted from my shoulders.

Carboneau had returned inside and I had ended up on his pallet. He was the first to greet me that morning, standing over me with that whiskered grin.

'Well, son, you've et enough to kill a horse and slept the better part of two days. You ready to get up and get on with your life?'

I returned his grin and stretched, only noticing as I began to rise that my moccasins, shirt and pants were gone. A new bandage covered the wound to my shoulder and I looked at him questioningly.

He cackled, nodding over his shoulder toward the shack. 'That Toby, she sure likes you. Took better care of you than a newborn babe! Had you stripped, washed and bandaged before you could say "scat".'

He cackled again at the look of discomfort that crossed my face. I had never been attended to before in such a fashion, at least not by a pretty young woman. He must have noticed my perplexity, as he slapped his thigh in contented merriment.

'Now, son, don't you be embarrassed. Womenfolk are put on this earth to look after us men. If'n they weren't, we'd've all died off long ago.'

He whistled then and thumped the side of the shack with his rifle butt. Toby appeared immediately, smiling sweetly at me. Still embarrassed, I looked away, and Carboneau chuckled again.

'Sweetie, bring this man his clothes, 'fore he wastes away from shame.'

Toby returned shortly with my clothes and turned her

back as I stepped into them gingerly. Once dressed, I explained everything that had transpired in the bayous, leaving out the more bloody specifics and the part about the lost chest of Jean Lafitte. Ring and Antoinette exchanged glances, but held their peace. Toby was just happy that I was back and that all this was finally over.

Ring was moving about pretty good, and I noticed that he had returned his knives to their previous locations – across his body. When I had recovered the gold from Frank Banks, I had discovered that Ring's knives had been taken from him and placed in the valise with the gold. Evidently Ring had made the same discovery.

I explained my intentions to everyone of pulling out in the morning. Carboneau assured me that he was well enough to travel, as had Ring, and I wanted to get out of here at first light.

Later, I pulled Carboneau aside and told him of my discovery. He looked at me dumbfounded, disbelief clear in his eyes. I had wedged the hasp in a fork in a tree when I had returned, and I showed it to him now. He held it with shaking fingers, tears welling up in his eyes.

'By God, son, this is it. I recognize the letters and the date, but had forgotten them until now. This is the very chest that I myself helped load into the boat. Where is it, son? Where's the chest now?'

'Come on, old man, I'll take you to it myself.'

We left together, presumably to recover the guns of Sawyer Bates and Hondo Cain, and to dispose of their bodies. No one questioned our intentions. I suppose they were too occupied thinking about our departure planned for tomorrow.

I led Carboneau right to the spot, and he looked on in wonder as I explained about the roots which had encircled the chest. Staying on dry land, he watched as I waded out to the submerged roots and began to work at freeing the chest.

187

We had brought a rope with us and I tied it securely around the chest, twice having to submerge myself completely underwater to accomplish my task.

Once the rope was secure, I tossed the end to Carboneau. He had to wade out in the water to catch the end and he held it anxiously now as I began to cut away at the roots with my knife. Finally, a passageway was cleared and I began to lift and tug on the chest in an effort to free it from the mud that reached at least halfway up its sides. It took some doing, as the chest was heavy, but at last it was free and we hauled her to shore.

She was easy to open as there was no lock to bar our way. The lid creaked a little at our intrusion, various bits of mud and debris tumbling to the ground.

The inside was full of mud and silt that had apparently worked itself inside over the long years of submersion. Carboneau dug away at its mass, using two hands as he scooped the mud out of its resting place and cast it impatiently to the forest floor.

I felt badly watching him labour away as it soon became obvious that there was nothing inside other than the mud that now lay scattered about haphazardly at his feet, and about fifty pounds of malleable lead that someone had dumped inside to weigh the chest down. A look of utter dejection and defeat crossed his face and he sat down heavily next to the chest that had been his pursuit for so many years.

It was heartbreaking to look at his face and I turned away, busying myself by examining the chest. At the very bottom, covered by the mud that disguised its identity, lay a small chain. I lifted it from its resting place and discovered that it was attached to a cross that was wedged into a crack at the bottom of the chest. Some gentle persuasive tugging freed it, and walking to the water's edge I carefully washed it clean.

It was a beautiful cross such as I had never seen before,

about two inches high and solid gold. In the centre was a bright shining red gem and it blinked at me translucently. This would be a ruby, I believed, and it was not the only gem to adorn the cross. Each of the four arms were embedded with gems of various colour; green, blue, purple and yellow, their arrangement forming a cross within a cross, with the larger ruby being the centrepiece.

The chain was sturdy yet delicate, and it too was of solid gold. The whole piece was a marvel to look at and its value would be beyond my wildest speculation. It looked as if it had been made for a queen or a princess in some far away land. As I marvelled at its beauty, Carboneau came up behind me.

'Beautiful, isn't it?' I said, standing up and handing it to him.

He took it and held it reverently in his muddy, shaking hands. A small reward for such a long search, but even his bitter disappointment was softened by its brilliantly crafted beauty.

'Keep it,' I said, 'you've earned it, and it's enough to start a new life.'

Toby had made us a lunch and we ate in silence. When we were through, I loaded the better part of the lead in the cloth that Toby had used to wrap our food. At Carboneau's questioning glance, I responded that I would use it for bullets, and he questioned me no further.

We returned quickly to our refuge, stopping only to gather the guns I had left behind with the bodies of Sawyer Bates and Hondo Cain. At our approach, Toby and Antoinette began preparing a meal. Carboneau ate glumly and at her glance, I only shrugged my shoulders.

I was the first up the following morning and I gathered the horses in preparation for our departure. I had them all saddled and loaded a half hour before anyone else was awake.

Our exodus was uneventful. Carboneau led the horses as before, the rest of us seated in the flatboat with our gear. The canoe was left behind as Toby had opted to ride with me.

Noon found us at the hut and Toby prepared a meal on their old potbellied stove. Old Man Carboneau and I waited outside, keeping an eye on the horses, which we had left saddled and ready to go. I asked him about his plans and what he planned to do now that his search for the lost chest of Lafitte was over.

'Why, son,' he replied, 'I don't want to be left behind.'

'What do you mean by that?' I asked, not understanding his meaning.

He turned and looked at me, peering at me intently, examining me as if something was wrong.

'What's the matter?' I asked, a bit apprehensively. 'Is something wrong?'

'Only your vision, son, and I had thought it fairly fine up until now.'

'What's wrong with my vision?'

'Why, that do beat all, young man. Can't you see that Toby's not going to let you go anywheres without her? That's what's wrong, son; your vision.'

At this bit of information, I swallowed uneasily, taking in the meaning of what he had said.

'I'm too old to be left behind, son. I reckon I'm going wherever y'all go, if you'll have me.'

With that settled and our bellies full again, we remounted and continued on. Twice I caught Ring and Antoinette looking at me surreptitiously and I rode warily near the valise that I had loaded on one of the extra horses, along with some odds and ends of blankets and useless gear.

When we reached the road that led on to New Orleans, I pulled up and at our prearranged signal, Old Man Carboneau moved off into the brush, ostensibly to answer a call of nature. I waited a moment until he was out of sight, then turned to Ring.

'Well, my friend,' I said, trying to affect a sense of sadness in my voice. 'I guess this is where we part company.'

He looked at me, a smile on his face, the rings by which he had earned his nickname glistening in the afternoon sun.

'*Oui, monsieur*, it is time to part.' His hand inched slightly toward his pistol and Antoinette's hand disappeared inside her handbag.

'I'm sure you can make it back to New Orleans on your own,' I said, smiling innocently at him. 'I appreciate all you've done for me. Will you be taking Antoinette with you?'

'*Oui, monsieur*, she will be accompanying me to New Orleans.'

I could see he was gauging his chances. He had seen me in action before and I didn't think he would risk it. The kicker was Antoinette. There was no telling what she would do.

Sensing the tension in our postures, Toby moved her horse closer to Antoinette's, flanking her on her right. Antoinette took notice and a look of exasperation turned her face ugly.

Just a moment longer, I thought. Just a moment more.

As if in answer to my silent plea, Old Man Carboneau bellowed from his place in the brush.

'Toby! Help me! Come quick!'

This was followed by a gunshot and Toby raced off into the brush to the aid of her grandfather. Glancing anxiously at Ring, I yelled my last command at him.

'Watch the horses! Something's happened to the old man!'

With that, I whirled Star around and spurred off into the brush. It took only a few moments to come upon Henry Carboneau. He sat upon his horse whispering into Toby's ear. He immediately led off and we fell in behind him. After a hundred yards, he fired another shot and followed suit, our shots winging harmlessly into the ground.

We began an arc then, swinging our way around and behind Ring and Antoinette, moving quietly now as we took up a position in a cluster of live oaks that hid us from sight yet gave us a clear view of the road back to New Orleans. Sure enough, not five minutes later, here came Ring and Antoinette, and they were just a-foggin' it up the road to New Orleans, the packhorse with the valise closely in tow.

Excitedly, Toby grabbed my arm pointing in desperation at Ring and Antoinette as they raced by.

'Look! Dot, they're getting away with the gold!'

She tugged desperately at my arm, yet I only turned and smiled, placing my hand over hers.

'Let them go. They deserve it, and they deserve each other.'

She looked at me as if I were daft, disbelief in her eyes.

'Dot, have you gone crazy? They have the gold! The gold that belongs to your friends!'

'Don't you worry about the gold, sweetie,' I said, squeezing her hand reassuringly and slapping my saddle-bags with my other hand. 'There ain't nothing but lead in that valise. All they'll make with that is a bunch of bullets.'

Old Man Carboneau laughed behind me and I smiled at Toby.

'By the time they know what happened to them, we'll be long gone. Gone to Texas,' I finished, squeezing Toby's hand again.

Old Man Carboneau cackled, slapping his thigh with his gnarled hand.

'Best damn thing I've heard in a long time, son – a long damn time. Gone to Texas!'